THE
DREAM
SNATCHER

Also by Annie Dalton

The Afterdark Princess
The Real Tilly Beany
Tilly Beany and the Best Friend Machine
Tilly Beany Saves the World

For older readers

The Alpha Box
Naming the Dark
Night Maze
Out of the Ordinary

THE
DREAM
SNATCHER

by Annie Dalton

Illustration by Lesley Harker

Mammoth

First published in Great Britain in 1998 by Mammoth,
an imprint of Reed International Books Limited,
Michelin House, 81 Fulham Road, London SW3 6RB

ISBN 0 7497 2977 5

10 9 8 7 6 5 4 3 2 1

A CIP catalogue record for this book
is available from the British Library

Typeset by Avon Dataset Ltd, Bidford on Avon, B50 4JH
Printed in Great Britain by Cox & Wyman Ltd,
Reading, Berkshire

With special thanks to my daughter Maria for her help with this book.
And to Christine, Joan, Viv and Dave for theirs.

Contents

1 Beware of the dream snatcher   1

2 Kevin nicks a cool jacket   10

3 Vampire alert   14

4 Leeks and lilies   25

5 Vasco's invisible zoo   39

6 The *Rusty Pineapple*   50

7 The humming-bird room   63

8 Girls can't fly   80

9 'Tickle tickle'   98

10 Finty's infallible skull dazzler 106

11 Through the Witches' Kitchen 126

12 Caught in a dream   141

13 The Pearl of the Deep   155

14 Kevin Kitchener's dream   173

1 Beware of the dream snatcher

Joe Quail was climbing a dream stairway. Below him, magical towers poked through a fading sunset. Above him, the stairs swooped and soared dizzily until they reached the stars.

The Princess of Afterdark was calling him. 'Where are you, Joe?'

'I'm coming,' he said sleepily.

At last Joe found her waiting on the highest stair of all, her wild hair blowing in the night sky. 'Who do you need me to fight this time? Trolls, dragons, evil enchanters?'

'No, Joe, it's your world which is in trouble now. And the danger is much closer than you think –'

But before she could explain, the air filled with terrible sighs. The stairway slowly cracked down the middle. As the half of the stair with the princess on it began to drift away, she cried, 'Wake up, Joe! Wake up, before it's too late!'

'No, wait! Take me with you!' shouted Joe.

There was another desolate sigh. Joe's stair started to crumble. He clutched at it to save himself, but the tiny shells it was made of broke off in his hand.

'Take care, Joe,' the princess cried faintly, as she floated into the night. 'Beware of the dream snatcher!'

But the stairs shattered into thousands of tiny pieces. Joe tumbled down through the stars, yelling at the top of his voice . . .

. . . And opened his eyes, his heart bumping wildly. Then he heard it again. The eerie sighing. Only this time it was right outside his window. He pulled back the curtain cautiously. Drifting towards him through the foggy dawn was a ghostly crowd of hot-air balloons.

Joe pinched himself in case he was still dreaming.

But the balloons were real, floating across the back gardens of Forest Street, and getting nearer every second. Now and then they gave gusty sighs as the balloonists controlled the flow of helium.

Joe usually loved hot-air balloons. They made him think of summer and circuses. But these balloons looked as if they'd been cut out of the fog. Even their swirling patterns were foggy. And the nearer they came, the darker it grew, until at last one balloon completely filled Joe's window with its shadow.

Joe flattened himself against the wall and tried not to breathe. *It knows I'm here.* For a terrified moment Joe thought the balloon was actually going to come crashing in through his window to get him. But at the last minute it veered sharply, like a driver avoiding broken glass. Then it nosed its way up the back of Joe's house and disappeared over the roof. Joe dived out of bed and tore out on to the landing, his heart hammering.

The balloon hung motionless outside Flora Neate's house. It's after snooty old Flora now, Joe thought, bewildered. From here he could see the balloonists in their fog-coloured clothes. One wore a hood, completely hiding his face. The other only looked to be in his teens, his wrists too lanky for his sleeves. He crouched over some kind of machine, fiddling with a few dials. Joe could see its keys glowing like unfriendly teeth.

'It's either a weird computer,' he muttered, 'or an even weirder musical instrument.'

The youth rippled his fingers along the keys. Joe caught his breath, half-expecting the street to fill with spooky music.

Instead there was silence, thick and cottony as a snowstorm.

The boy's fingers skimmed over the keys, gently smoothing away all the tiny ordinary sounds of the everyday world. First he blotted out the street sounds. Soon the hum of the fridge downstairs was gone, then the gurgle of the pipes in the airing cupboard, until the only sound left in the street was Joe's scared breathing.

The youth twiddled a new dial and began to play a song without words or melody. But it wasn't meant to be listened to. This song was meant to be *felt*, Joe thought, as warm delicious feelings swooped and surged along the street like gypsy violins. It was softer than the softest lullaby, sweeter than lemon pie, irresistible as moonlight. 'Come to me,' it implored. 'I'd never hurt you. Please don't hide. I've waited so long. I'm lonely without you.'

The man in the hood stepped forward and made a caressing movement with his hand. Joe caught his breath as a starry net flew gracefully through the air and stuck itself to Flora Neate's window, like a spider's

4

web. With the skill of a snake-charmer, the hooded figure reeled his glittering net back in, careful not to spill his mysterious catch.

Joe strained on tiptoe, his heart thudding, desperate to see what was in the net. The man seemed astonished at it, whatever it was. He gave an impatient thumbs-down signal. The balloon moved off again, sighing its way along the street, house by house, until finally it drew level with a small cracked window. Kevin Kitchener's room. With a hiccup, the balloon stopped and hung in the air, wheezing painfully.

Joe swallowed. The balloonists were after his friend, Kevin, and there wasn't a thing he could do.

Then the musician played his lemon-pie lullaby love song, and the sinister figure threw his starry net at the boxroom window and reeled it back. This time Joe saw what he caught in it.

Nothing at all.

Abruptly, the balloon lifted itself high over the narrow houses of Forest Street. And for the first time the pattern decorating the now-speeding balloon came into focus.

And it wasn't a pattern. It was words.

In swirling magician's writing, Joe read:

Dream Snatchers
Grand Opening Saturday Night

A wave of relief washed over him. It was a publicity stunt all the time! Joe almost danced back to his room.

Dream Snatchers was the new games arcade being built at the end of Forest Street. Joe passed it on his way to school. Kevin's brother Jason worked there. It was enormous inside, Kevin said. Eye-boggling, mind-dazzling rooms of machines and games so new they'd never been played before anywhere in the world.

The owner of Dream Snatchers had a glamorous name, which Joe found hard to keep in his head. Vasco, that was it. Vasco Shine. Mostly everyone called him Vee, as if he was their favourite big brother, not their boss at all.

He drove a sleek pearly car the colour of moonlight. The odd-looking hound which followed him everywhere was pearly too. Vee was a zillionaire already, Kevin said, even though he was hardly any older than Jason. That's why he was so successful, that's how Vee knew what children and teenagers liked, what thrilled them, what their deepest secrets were; because he was still young himself.

But although Vee was young, he never stopped working, never took a holiday, not even one day off. He hardly even slept, Kevin said.

Vee had high standards for his staff too. If you didn't

do things right, no matter how sorry you were, there was no second chance. One mistake and, in the nicest possible way, you were out on your ear.

What Joe had seen was just a secret rehearsal for tomorrow's big opening. Now the whole thing made perfect sense. Dizzy with relief he slid back under his quilt. His room was unexpectedly cold. Joe pulled the quilt right over his head, shivering, and promptly fell asleep again. This time there were no dreams waiting for him.

By morning Joe was sleeping so deeply it took his mum several goes to wake him. 'It's foggy again,' she grumbled, peering out of his window. She'd slept badly too. It was lucky the phone went, or she'd have been late for work. They rushed around frazzled.

Then, just as his mum was doing her mascara, she sprang her surprise. 'Which do you want, Joe? The good news or the bad news? Don't worry,' she added, 'you'll go wild when I tell you the good news. And the bad news isn't really bad.'

'The good news, then,' he said cheerfully.

His mum beamed at him in the mirror. 'Alice Fazackerley is babysitting tonight.'

'Wow!' yelled Joe, spraying toast crumbs. 'Why didn't you say?'

'I didn't know till the phone rang just now. Angela and her husband have both gone down with flu and she's offered me their theatre tickets. We've got to leave early, so Alice will meet you outside school.'

Joe had stopped listening. The wonderful words were chasing round his head. *Alice Fazackerley's coming tonight*. He'd been longing to hear them for months.

'Oh,' Joe remembered, putting on his coat. 'You never told me the bad news.'

His mum's smile wavered. 'I've invited Flora's dad to come to the theatre with me. But the baby isn't very well. Tom thought it would be best if Alice babysat for the three of you at his house.'

'Are you *crazy*?'

'But their father's such a sweet man,' said his mother helplessly. 'It must be hard bringing up those little girls by himself. It would do him good to go out and relax. And there's two of them and only one of you, Joe. It's much easier for –'

'But Flora's a weirdo, Mum, and Tat's only a baby.'

'What *difference* does it make?'

'What difference?' yelled Joe, working himself into a fury. 'Only that you've ruined everything. That's all.'

He stormed upstairs and flung himself on his bed. Then he hurled his pillow across the room, sending a model troll flying. 'Flora Neate,' he snarled. 'If she was any paler she'd be totally invisible.' Except for her weird eyes, he remembered with a shudder of dislike. They were so dark they were practically navy. It wasn't just Joe who thought she was weird. All his friends did. When the Neates moved in, his mum had dragged him over to be neighbourly. But Flora just took herself into a corner with a book and munched her way through a bag of lurid raspberry jellies.

'And she didn't offer me *one*,' he muttered. 'Even I was never as weird as that.' He sighed. The truth was, Joe had been fairly weird, the kind of boy who was scared of everything. Then one day teenage Alice came to babysit and took him to the kingdom of Afterdark where she was the last princess. And by the time his adventures were over Joe had almost got the hang of being a hero.

'Alice Fazackerley,' Joe murmured.

And a shiver of pure happiness went through him.

2 Kevin nicks a cool jacket

On the other side of Forest Street, Kevin Kitchener was hunting for Archie. Thanks to their shared adventures in Afterdark, Kevin's bullying days were over. He and Joe Quail were now the best of friends. But even Joe wasn't as important to Kevin as his scruffy little dachshund.

Kevin couldn't understand it. When he fell asleep in front of the horror film, the little dog had been sprawled comfortably next to him. But just as it was getting light, a horrible wheezing filled the room, so that he shot upright on the sofa in a panic. And behind his knees where Archie should have been was a dreadful space.

Kevin searched the downstairs rooms softly, so as not to wake his mum. Jason worked most nights for Dream Snatchers now, so Kevin didn't worry about him. But Archie wasn't hopefully polishing his empty bowl, or raiding the bin.

He crept upstairs and peered into his own room without much hope. It felt colder than usual, its single curtain flapping like a broken wing. 'Archie,' he hissed, desperate for Archie to wriggle out guiltily from his hiding place, and start fussing over Kevin. But he didn't.

He didn't know what to do. He opened the airing cupboard in case Archie had got shut in by mistake. But there was only a bunch of ratty old towels.

Jason locked his door whenever he went out, so there was no point checking the attic. Kevin's sister Karen had left home months ago. Both Kevin and Archie avoided her room. Without his sister's big red heart-cushions and her country-and-western collection, her room looked as if the burglars had been in. Kevin's mum was threatening to get lodgers.

That left one other room in the house. So in case, for the first time in history, Archie was having a nice

11

snooze with the woman who wished him dead, Kevin turned the handle and crept into the heavy-breathing darkness. But his mum was snoring alone. Kevin's throat began to ache, as if a bone had got stuck there without him knowing. 'Mum, Archie's gone,' he said huskily.

The bedspread surged upward then fell back with a groan. 'Go to school,' it mumbled. 'And don't forget your key this time.'

Kevin backed unhappily through the door. Then he tried again. 'Mum, I heard a noise in the night. Sort of horrible breathing. What if it scared him? What if Archie never comes back?' His voice shook.

'You watch too much telly,' sneered a voice. 'You've given yourself bad dreams.' It was Jason. He took the stairs to his room in three lanky strides and shut himself in with a slam.

'How can I sleep with this row?' shrieked Kevin's mum.

Kevin closed her door. 'I don't dream, Jay,' he whispered. 'If you want to know. Real life is horrible enough, thanks.'

Then he noticed Jason's big jacket draped over the stairs. Jason had worn it ever since he started working for Dream Snatchers. But Jason had recently shot up again, so he was getting a new one. Vee's employees had to look right, Jason explained, if Dream

Snatchers was going to rake in the money.

Kevin wished he was old enough to work for Vee. He stroked the soft lining jealously. It was as warm as a new lamb. But, on the outside, the huge grey jacket was all cool, streetwise wolf.

He lifted it down. It was like hugging a big cloud. 'Thanks, Jay,' he murmured, slipping his arms into the sleeves. 'Gets nippy, looking for lost dogs in the fog.'

His reflection stared back warily from the hall mirror. Kevin grinned with surprise. He looked bigger, meaner. No one could hurt him now, he thought, not wearing a coat like this. He hesitated, then, pulling the hood firmly over his head, Kevin jogged out through the door and into the foggy street.

3 Vampire alert

Joe's mind whirled with a confused mixture of excitement and gloom as he walked to school. Then, just as he passed Dream Snatchers, unusually silent behind its wooden cladding, he heard footsteps pounding along behind him. 'Oi – Joe Quail!' someone yelled.

Swinging round, Joe found himself face to face with a dangerous-looking kid in a hooded jacket. Then the boy grinned the grin that once struck fear into Joe's heart and he started breathing again. It was only Kevin.

'I didn't recognise you,' said Joe. He wasn't so relieved as he should have been. Kevin's jacket reminded him disturbingly of his dawn terrors.

'My new image,' beamed Kevin. 'Like the jacket?' he asked chattily, as they jogged down the shortcut to Golden Street School. 'I nicked it off Jay. He won't miss it, he's getting a new one. You're late, aren't you?'

'I overslept,' said Joe, unwilling to go into more detail.

'Do us a favour, then. Tell Miss Field you were helping me look for Archie? If I tell her she'll think it's one of those my-aardvark-ate-my-homework-Miss excuses.' Kevin grinned again, but Joe saw misery at the back of his eyes. 'Can you believe it?' Kevin demanded, 'I've been calling him till I'm hoarse.'

'When did he go?' asked Joe.

'He was there when I fell asleep and when I woke he was gone – like into thin air.'

'Listen,' said Joe urgently. 'I'm really sorry about Archie but Alice is babysitting for me tonight. At Flora Neate's house. Don't ask,' he said, seeing Kevin break into his famous shark's grin. 'But, Kevin –'

Before Joe could ask Kevin to come along for moral support, the headmaster billowed through the front door of Golden Street School, waving impatiently.

'Hurry up,' shouted Mr Bird. 'I'm surprised at *you*, Joe,' he added as Kevin and Joe panted up the steps.

'I warned him there'd be the odd straggler,' he added, somehow managing to glare at Kevin and pat Joe's shoulder at the same time. 'Fortunately he just phoned to say he's running late. This fog is causing chaos everywhere.'

'Who's running late?' Joe asked, baffled.

'Mr Shine, of course,' beamed the headmaster. 'Everyone's waiting for him in the hall. They've even sent someone from the radio station. Local hero shares success. Such a role model for you all. You might learn a thing or two,' he added sharply to Kevin.

'Mr Shine?' Joe repeated. 'Coming here? You don't mean *Vasco* Shine?' He had another twinge of unease.

'Here he comes,' carolled Mr Bird. He pattered down the steps as a moonlight-coloured limousine slid almost soundlessly through the gates.

Kevin tugged Joe's sleeve. 'Better find Miss Field,' he said urgently. 'Face the music, eh?'

The car purred to a halt in the visitors' parking bay.

'Wait,' said Joe. Suddenly Joe badly needed to see Vasco Shine for himself.

A pretty girl climbed out first, clutching a tiny handbag.

'Welcome, welcome,' called Mr Bird.

'Vee mustn't see me wearing this,' begged Kevin. He seemed genuinely scared.

'Hang *on*,' insisted Joe.

16

The driver's door opened. Joe glimpsed a crisp jacket cuff, a male wrist with the faintest sheen of suntan. Then a heavy glint of silver.

But there was no time to wonder about these things, because now Vee himself was bounding across the playground like a youth in a vitamin commercial. 'Sorry I'm late,' he cried. 'This is my assistant, Vermilion.'

'Now!' hissed Kevin, dragging Joe into school.

The corridor was empty. So was the cloakroom.

Kevin shrugged himself desperately out of the jacket, found a cupboard full of football boots, stuffed the coat in and jammed the door shut, micro-seconds before Mr Bird pattered back in.

'If you wouldn't mind wearing these badges,' Mr Bird was saying apologetically. 'And could you jot down your car number plate? Security, you know.'

'Of course,' said Vee pleasantly. 'Safety first.' But something about the way he said it told Joe that Vee was secretly laughing at their headmaster with his fussy ways.

'Oh, they're still here, my little stragglers,' beamed Mr Bird, shepherding Joe and Kevin towards the hall. 'I'm sure Miss Field will forgive them this once,' he said fondly.

Kevin crossed his eyes with disgust.

As they reached the hall Joe heard an expectant

17

hum. All the juniors were in there, packed tightly together like little factory chickens; absolutely dying to see the famous owner of Dream Snatchers.

'Over here – quickly,' commanded Miss Field. Joe slid into a space. Kevin did his old man's leer. 'Your girlfriend's waiting, Quail,' he said, giving him a nudge.

Joe glanced at his neighbour long enough to register a glimmering wing of pale hair, a flowery sleeve and a pale, pointy little face. Flora Neate. Her expression was even stonier than usual, he noticed. His heart sank at the thought of a whole evening with her.

Then Vee bounded in, whipped off his sunglasses, turned on the full beam of his boyish smile and Joe forgot his disappointment. He forgot everything.

Vee was wonderful. It wasn't just how he looked. That perfectly ordinary jacket over the even more ordinary T-shirt; the cropped black hair that glinted almost blue under the lights. It wasn't even anything Vee said. Something about being a poor kid in a poor family but still believing in the magic of dreams. It was Vee himself. The healthy gleam and glow of him. The way energy came crackling out of those fine sensitive hands. His warm, infectious laugh. The way he seemed to be talking specially to Joe, like a loving older brother. Even his constant fiddling with that old-fashioned silver pocket watch he had, like a restless little kid; snapping it open, glancing inside and shutting it again.

As if underneath it all, and despite being so famous, Vee was rather shy.

The door creaked open. A damp nose edged round it, followed by a droopy silk tassle of an ear.

'Aah,' said all the lower juniors, enchanted.

The weirdest dog in the world crept into the hall. By the time she reached Vermilion's chair, the skinny creature was trembling all over. The girl leaned down. 'Lulu,' she whispered. 'Behave.' At once the dog began to fold up her great awkward stalks of legs, cramming her hind quarters obediently under the chair, until only her huge head was visible, resting mournfully on Vermilion's knees. But her great scared eyes were fixed only on Vee.

'Aah,' said the lower juniors again. And, resting their chins in their hands, they gazed adoringly at Vee too.

Vee made Joe feel weak with envy. And Kevin was so overwhelmed at being in the same room as his hero, he'd practically stopped breathing.

But on Joe's other side, Flora started to fidget. Then she yawned. 'Nice folding-dog trick,' she murmured in a bored voice. 'He's got her so scared, the poor beast thinks she's a deckchair.'

'She's not scared, stupid, she's just pedigree,' Joe corrected her, scowling. 'Vee's brilliant.'

Somehow Flora had dragged Joe out of a delicious

dream he hadn't realised he was having. All his nerves jangled as though she'd scraped her nails down the blackboard.

'Brilliant? Is that what you call him?' snorted Flora. 'I thought children were meant to be safe in school. Mr Bird should be sounding a vampire alert. Not giving them security badges.'

Joe's jaw dropped. '*What* did you say?' he mouthed.

'Who else do you think would go creeping around the rooftops with a big glittery net?' muttered Flora fiercely. 'I'd have thought it was obvious to anyone with half a brain. He's a dream vampire, you idiot. He's swagged hundreds of children's dreams already. It's lucky I was waiting for him,' she added with a grim little smile.

'That was just a stunt for Dream Snatchers,' began Joe. But, suddenly, his dawn terrors came flooding back. That's why Alice wanted me to wake up, he thought, before Vasco could charm my dreams into his net too. 'But she didn't tell me he was a *vamp* –' Flora clapped her hand furiously across his mouth and his sentence ended in a startled squawk.

'Sssh,' hissed Miss Field.

'Idiot,' breathed Flora. 'Can't you see what he's doing to them all?'

Chillingly wide awake now, Joe began to pay close attention. Vee saw Flora's disapproval at once, he noticed, but he didn't seem to mind. He just went on talking, flashing Flora the occasional brotherly grin. But, as Joe watched, Vee started to change. He grew twice as handsome. And everything he said was so funny! Vasco Shine was radiant with charm. *If only you'd trust me*, he seemed to be pleading. *See what fun we'd have*? He clicked his watch open, and glanced inside, looking terribly young and in need of a friend. Any normal girl would melt in the tropical sunlight of Vasco Shine, Joe thought. But Flora just kept smiling her grim crooked little smile. And all at once Joe understood.

Vasco Shine had everyone under a charm spell, teachers and children alike. The only person in the hall who wasn't doing what Vee wanted was Flora Neate. Now, thanks to her, nor was Joe. And something odd happened. Vee faltered and seemed to lose his thread. The lower juniors started fidgeting and rubbing their eyes. Then Joe heard someone at the back of the hall give a loud yawn and someone else had a fit of nervous giggles. One by one the children stirred and stared about them, bewildered. They all looked exhausted.

As if it wasn't bad enough for Vasco Shine to steal their dreams, thought Joe disgustedly. But he had to make children *love* him too.

Abruptly Vee began to wind things up. 'That's quite

21

enough from me, kids,' he said humorously. 'Let's cut straight to the car chase. Miss Field, tell them the news!'

Vee gave Joe's teacher a flirty smile but there was a kind of bored cruelty in it now. As if Golden Street School had let him down so badly, he couldn't be bothered to hide his contempt.

'Oh, yes,' said Miss Field, getting to her feet. She flushed unhappily. 'To celebrate the opening of his exciting new – enterprise, Mr Shine has generously donated new sports equipment to the school,' she stammered. 'Also some small gifts for you to take home. May we have some strong boys to carry everything in.'

Joe and Kevin were chosen. The prospect of presents gave the tired children a new lease of energy and they surged out into the foggy playground, screaming with excitement.

Flora followed slowly, her navy blue eyes inscrutable.

Vee raced ahead with his car keys. When the boot flew up and the children saw all the boxes stacked inside, everyone fell silent again.

'Vee's car even *smells* expensive,' said someone wonderingly.

'Take it away, take it all,' said Vee with his warm laugh. But it was obvious to everyone now that he was dying to speed away and do something more exciting than hang about with a bunch of boring little kids.

Then another odd thing happened. Vee gave Kevin one of the heaviest boxes to carry. And when Kevin staggered, trying to balance it, Vee placed a steadying arm round his shoulders, and murmured something in his ear. Kevin scowled and ducked his head, as if he was trying not to cry. Vee whispered something else and after a few seconds, Joe saw Kevin nod a nearly invisible 'yes'. Then Vee caught Joe looking. 'That's quite a stare,' he said. 'Think you'll recognise me if we meet again?' But this time his amused expression had a glint of menace in it. Joe flushed and started to lug his cartons of sportswear across the playground.

Mr Bird cried hopefully, 'You will stay for coffee?'

Vee, completely unsmiling now, clicked his pocket watch open, glanced inside and shut it one last time. 'Sorry, gotta run, everyone,' he said coolly. 'Tomorrow is our big day.' Seconds later, the car was pulling away. The children waved with the stunned expressions of orphans. A vicious fight broke out between a couple of older boys over the possession of one of the boxes. One of the junior girls burst into floods of tears.

'What's the matter?' asked Miss Field, who looked strangely upset herself.

'I don't know,' the girl wailed hysterically. 'I want to go home.'

Then a small boy shrieked, 'Wait! He's slowing down!'

The driver's window slid down and someone with the faintest glint of suntan scattered exuberant handfuls of Dream Snatchers vouchers into the air.

Everyone went wild. All the children scrambled over each other, frantic to grab the fluttering scraps of paper before they blew away.

All except for Flora. She ignored Vee's rain of moonlit magic money. She ignored the balloons and badges. She ignored the plumes of exhaust swirling round her ankles, like a genie's vapour trail.

Joe followed her gaze, puzzled. And then he saw what everyone else had been dazzled into missing.

The scared-looking boy crouching down in the back of Vee's car. Vasco Shine had kidnapped Kevin.

4   Leeks and lilies

Joe kept trying to tell Miss Field about Vasco Shine really being a vampire and kidnapping Kevin, but alarmingly she couldn't seem to see or hear him.

It was the same with the other teachers. No one noticed Kevin Kitchener was missing. It was as if he'd never existed.

When lunch-time came, Joe gloomily swirled a fork through his cottage pie, unable to swallow a mouthful.

Flora slid on to the chair opposite and began to

nibble one of her revolting beetroot sandwiches. 'It's not all their fault,' she murmured. 'He's fixed it so they don't know. And we can't tell.'

The afternoon went on for ever. Finally, when Joe was almost too tired and miserable to care, the bell rang and everyone spilled out of the classroom. Flora flitted up as he was getting his coat. 'Coming?' she said in his ear.

Joe clutched his heart. 'Don't *do* that.'

'Hurry, Joe,' she pleaded. 'Alice is waiting.'

Joe stared. Flora didn't even know Alice. Why was she so excited?

'My baby sister's not well,' said Flora quickly, her pale face flushing. 'Fog is bad for her chest. Come on!' Joe raced after her.

Walking towards them, looking as calm and sensible as if vampires had never been invented, was Alice Fazackerley. She was wearing her plush brown coat and her well-polished second-best boots. She'd pulled a soft tammy over her ears and her hair hung down in one shining chestnut plait. She was pushing a buggy with an extremely pale baby in it. In her hand she carried a basket of groceries. And she looked so beautiful, dear and utterly real, Joe couldn't say a single word.

'Hiya, Tat,' said Flora, kissing the baby, whose dreadful real name, Joe knew, was Titania.

26

The little girl scrubbed the kisses away irritably. 'Nyeugh stoppit. Bite you bite you,' she shrieked, her baby teeth gleaming like pointy pearls in the dusk. Then she coughed, a tiny barking cough.

'Hello, Joe,' said Alice, giving him a quick hug. Her hair smelled of frost and shampoo. 'And you're Flora,' she said to Flora. 'Are you as fierce as little Tat?'

'Not really,' said Flora shyly. Her weird navy blue eyes met Alice's steady grey ones and such a long look passed between them that Joe almost choked with jealousy.

The baby twisted round to explore the shopping. 'Bread bread,' she chanted. 'Bite it bite it.'

'Alice, what are these leeks for?' Flora asked politely.

'I thought we needed some filling soup,' said Alice. 'Leeks will be good for the baby's cold.'

It was weird. Now Alice was finally here, Joe didn't know what to say. Too many strange things had happened. Not once upon a time in a faraway king-dom, but today, in Joe's own world. Sinister balloons, a dream-snatching vampire. And now a terrifying kidnapping. And what was Alice talking about? *Soup*! It made Joe feel slightly crazy. He stumbled on a paving stone. When he looked up again, what he saw was so magical, that if it wasn't for the cars and

27

shivering passers-by, he could almost believe they had slipped into Alice's kingdom already.

The builders' cladding had gone. In its place floated a dreamlike structure of smoky glass, a fabulous palace pouring with light and sound. And over the door, in swirling magician's letters, was the name DREAM SNATCHERS.

Joe squinted in anxiously, hoping to catch a glimpse of Kevin. 'This wasn't built by builders,' Joe muttered. 'Vasco did it with magic, bet you anything you like.'

'Hurry, Joe,' Alice called. 'We've got that soup to make.'

Soup again! What was wrong with Alice? 'You don't understand,' Joe began. 'Kevin's been –'

'Not here, Joe,' said Alice firmly. And he realised that Alice knew only too well what had happened to Kevin.

Alice began threading her way through a lively gang of girls and young men. They were unloading a van, laughing, flirting and tossing boxes to one another. Jason stood nearby, scribbling on a clipboard. Joe wondered if he knew his brother had been kidnapped by a vampire.

Then, to his horror, Joe saw Vasco Shine a few metres ahead of them, handing out lilies to female passers-by. He had changed into a new set of ordinary but, somehow, dazzlingly perfect clothes. He looked three times as handsome as he had done at Joe's school and was fizzing with party spirit.

'Cross over, Alice,' Joe hissed. 'It's the vampire.'

As if she hadn't heard, Alice went on pushing Tat's buggy sturdily up the street.

A flattered young mum accepted her long-stemmed flower, blushing. 'Bye, sweetheart,' Vee called after her. 'Bring the whole family along tomorrow to our grand opening.'

'Alice,' pleaded Joe.

Alice stopped dead. 'Congratulations,' she said. 'You must be proud.'

She doesn't mean it, thought Joe. She *can't*.

'Thank you,' said Vee smoothly. 'May I give you this flower with the compliments of Dream Snatchers?' He selected a fresh lily and held it out with a flourish, the way an actor might.

Then he seemed to see Alice for the first time. 'It's you,' he said, his voice husky with surprise. 'How are you?' he added quickly. 'I didn't recognise you. It's been – *how* long has it been?'

'You haven't changed a bit,' said Alice without a glimmer of a smile. 'Still disgustingly charming. Still scheming to take over any world you're passing through.'

'I try to make the best of my opportunities,' said Vee lightly.

29

'Does that include kidnapping children?' asked Alice.

Vee looked hurt. 'Really, Alice, kidnapping. I simply borrowed Kevin to help us with some last-minute preparations. With the full co-operation of Mrs Kitchener and the school authorities who thought it was a wonderful opportunity for him. Now please, won't you take this flower, for old times' sake?' And as he held out the lily again, his voice grew lullaby soft and sweet as lemon pie.

The lily's petals flared in the dusk like light from a star.

Joe watched, hypnotised, as Vee's and Alice's hands moved towards each other, almost touching.

Suddenly, the door of Dream Snatchers burst open and Vee's weird dog hurtled out, howling like a werewolf.

Flora threw her arms protectively round Tat.

'Dog dog dog,' shrieked Tat, stretching her own short arms as wide as they would go. 'Bite you bite you!' She gnashed her tiny teeth, coughing with excitement.

But Lulu was only interested in one person. And when she saw her she stopped her bloodcurdling howls and skidded to a standstill, with one ear inside out and the other sticking up like a question mark.

Then, whimpering softly, as if she was afraid she

might be dreaming, Vee's dog crept forward and laid her head reverently on Alice Fazackerley's second-best boots.

'Well, Alice is the Lady of the Beasts in her own world,' said Joe, blinking hard.

'I know,' Flora told him, with her snooty smile.

'But *how* do you know?' Joe was in despair. It drove him wild the way Flora kept knowing things, and how she and Alice were such instant girly chums, shutting Joe out.

Flora frowned. 'It's hard to explain.' And she never got the chance, because right in the middle of the high street, Alice knelt down, stroking Lulu's silky ears.

'Poor Luna,' she murmured tenderly. 'What has he done to you?' When she looked up again, Joe shivered. He'd never seen Alice angry before. 'Must you have everything you set your heart on, Vasco Shine?' she blazed at him.

'It's not my fault,' said Vee sulkily. 'I feed Lulu well enough.'

'Her name is Luna,' cried Alice. 'She's pining for her home.'

'She loves me,' said Vee. 'Ask these kids.' He fiddled nervously with his silver pocket watch.

'It's her nature,' said Alice. 'She can't help herself.' She bent her head, whispering in Luna's ear.

31

The dog made questioning sounds down her nose.

'I promise,' said Alice in a clear voice. 'If all goes well, you'll only have to bear it a little longer.'

Luna scrambled to her feet, her claws slipping on the pavement, and padded back to Vee's side. But her shining eyes never left Alice.

'I don't think I will have that flower,' said Alice, giving Vee one last cool stare. 'Let's go,' she said to the children. 'This fog is bad for the baby's cough.'

'Do you think I never get homesick?' Vee called after her. 'Don't you think I long for freedom? I'd do anything to have that sweet life back. You could help me, Alice. You could help me go back home.' His voice cracked with emotion.

'Goodbye, Vee,' said Alice, walking away.

Vee flung the remaining lilies on the ground. 'You'll be sorry,' he yelled furiously. 'I always get what I set my heart on, you said so yourself. You're against me, like all the others. With or without your help, I'll get back into Afterdark. Then you'll be sorry!'

They walked the rest of the way to Flora's house in silence. Once they were safely indoors, Alice gave baby Tat a carrot to keep her teeth busy, and unpacked the shopping.

'You two scrub and peel,' she said briskly. 'And I'll chop and cook. Is that fair?'

No, thought Joe. It's crazy. He knew Alice was wonderful and everything, but tonight she seemed to have vegetable soup on the brain.

'Shouldn't we get going?' he objected. 'I mean, did you realise Vasco Shine actually came to our school? He put a vampire spell on everyone and then he kidnapped Kevin but no one believes us. Everyone else thinks Vasco Shine is the bee's knees. They don't understand about vampires and magic. We've got to go to Afterdark and *make* someone help us. We haven't got time to make some old soup!'

Alice smiled. 'Don't you remember any of the rules of being an outlaw, Joe?' she teased him.

Joe grinned back. This was the first time Alice had even hinted at their adventures in Afterdark. 'You mean that stuff about making a good stew. But there's no time,' he pleaded again. 'It's almost dark already.'

'Here's the deal, Joe. You help with the tea and I'll take care of time. Worrying never solved anything. Home-made soup, on the other hand, solves practically everything. That's a joke,' she explained.

'OK,' said Joe uncertainly.

'Besides,' said Alice, 'now you're right in the middle of a new quest, you need something to put heart into you.'

Joe's heart began to pound. 'In the middle of a – do you mean it's already *started*? Here in this world?'

'It started the moment you woke and heard the balloon outside your window.'

He gazed at her, amazed. 'I didn't know quests could start in this world.'

'Oh, but they always do, Joe,' said Alice softly. 'They start here and they end here. And that's how it's always been.'

'Can I ask something, Alice?' said Flora in a small voice. 'It's been worrying me all the way home.' She looked terribly pale, even for Flora.

'Of course.'

'Well,' said Flora bravely, 'please, do you mind leaving the leeks out of your soup, because I really, really hate them a lot. Sorry.'

Later, while the soup simmered (two kinds, one with leeks, one without), Alice took Tat upstairs to have her bath. Flora and Joe drifted into the sitting-room. There wasn't much in it, except some armchairs, a big old colour TV and shelves crammed with books, some of them written by Flora's dad.

Joe fiddled shyly with the photographs. Most of them were snaps of Tat and Flora looking deadly pale in a variety of flowery dresses. There was one of Flora's dad too, at his typewriter. Bobbing around on his head, like the feelers of a giant insect, was a pair of deeny boppers. Weirdness obviously ran in the family.

'They're idea-catchers,' Flora explained. 'I made

them for when Dad gets writer's block.'

'Do they help?' asked Joe with interest.

Flora rolled her eyes. 'Why else would he wear them?'

'He looks as if he's forgotten he's got them on.'

'He forgets everything when he's writing,' sighed Flora, looking glum.

Another photograph caught Joe's eye. A pale woman with navy blue eyes. Joe guessed she was Flora's mother who died not long after Tat was born. Flora sighed again and switched the TV on and they watched children's programmes until tea was ready.

Flora shook a red blizzard of chilli pepper over her soup before she ate it, but Alice didn't mind. Then Alice coaxed Tat to take her cough medicine, and after that she sang a lullaby in a voice so soft Joe could never quite catch the words through the kitchen door, though he did try.

Just as Joe was teaching Flora how to blow huge bubbles with washing-up liquid, Alice came in. 'It's time,' she said.

'Time to – to go *there*, you mean?' Joe spluttered.

'Quickly,' said Alice. 'My friends will be here any minute.' And she ran lightly up the stairs with the baby in her arms. Somehow, on the way up, her hair came undone, tumbling loose in a shining storm.

It's happening, thought Joe, his mouth dry. But, by

the time Joe and Flora reached the landing, Alice and the baby had mysteriously vanished.

'Where have they –?' Joe began.

'The attic!' panted Flora.

The light bulb was broken. Joe and Flora groped their way up the stairs in darkness. But the attic too was empty.

'She must be out there,' said Flora uncertainly. She pointed to a low door creaking slightly on its hinges. Joe dived through it and found himself plunged into fog so thick that he stopped dead in a panic. Flora came after him, shivering. 'I can't see them,' she wailed.

A gust of wind tore the fog into wreathing scarves. For an instant there was a swirling gap. And there, safe and sound like a picture in a swirly frame, were Alice and the baby, with chimneys on either side of them, like giant kings.

Joe and Flora fled across the tiles before the fog could come boiling back. Flora flattened herself against a chimney stack and closed her eyes. 'Maybe we could hold hands,' she suggested. 'So we know where everyone is. Just an idea.'

Tat loved the roof. 'Dark dark dark,' she sang. She wriggled one arm free from the blanket.

'Alice, did I tell you that I don't actually like heights?' asked Flora in her politest voice.

Alice peered through the fog. 'I can't think where they –'

A mighty rushing drowned her words as something invisible came roaring high over the rooftops like a battering wind, bringing a blast of heat so fierce it almost knocked Joe off his feet.

Had Alice summoned dragons to carry them into Afterdark? he wondered fearfully. But a powerful fragrance drifted through the air; sweet, strange, yet hauntingly familiar.

'At last,' said Alice.

Then a sigh floated over the rooftops; so faint Joe hardly noticed it. But Flora looked round sharply, her pale hair swinging across her face. She whispered to Alice.

'It's all right, I'll get him,' murmured the princess. She tucked Tat's arm back inside the blanket and bundled her into Flora's arms.

'What's happening?' asked Joe, alarmed.

'Change of plan,' said Alice. She squeezed Joe's hand. There was tingling magic in her touch. His hand felt so comfortable in hers that he allowed her to draw him gently out of the shelter of the chimney stacks, until they stood at the very edge of the roof, like birds getting ready to fly. Alice brushed her fingers lightly across the back of Joe's neck. This time, not just Joe's hand but his whole self tingled with enchantment.

37

I always feel so safe with Alice, Joe thought dreamily, I'm not even cold any more.

Somewhere far off, Flora and Alice were discussing someone. 'Are you sure he'll be OK?' Flora was asking.

'Don't worry,' said Alice. 'Someone will meet him there.'

Then Alice sounded alarmingly near again. 'One, two, three!' she cried in a ringing voice. And she pushed Joe off the roof.

Down he fell and down, too shocked and betrayed to make a sound.

As he plummeted through the fog, he felt the rush and scorch of invisible wings. He heard confused cries overhead, he heard the shriek of the wind and the desolate sigh of a hot-air balloon.

But drowning out everything was the warm triumphant laugh of Vasco Shine.

5 Vasco's invisible zoo

Vital bits of Kevin's terrifying day kept going missing. For instance, the exact moment when Vasco Shine's pearly limousine mysteriously turned into a lift of smoked glass and went humming to the top of the Dream Snatchers building.

After that he did remember being surprised by Vee's office. Apart from the fresh lilies on the desk and a mirror with too many reflections in it, the room was as austere as a hardware store.

Vee was prowling up and down like a big cat in a cage. 'You're a thief, Kevin,' he'd whispered right in front of all the kids at school. Then he'd said, 'You wouldn't want your brother to lose his job.'

But even though Kevin knew it was stupid, even while Vee was kidnapping him, he kept hoping Vee would turn back into the friendly big brother he had been before. Maybe give him a bit of a talking to, Kevin wouldn't mind that, then buy Kevin a double chocolate milkshake and turn him loose in Dream Snatchers to have free goes on all those machines.

Instead Kevin was staring down over the foggy town, sweating with panic, as Vee bellowed on about everyone in his life who'd ever let him down. It was only a matter of time before Vee remembered where Kevin Kitchener's name was on that list. 'The way that odd little girl looked *through* me,' Vee was saying in a hurt voice. 'It was going perfectly until then. I mean, do I look like a monster to you?'

Kevin swallowed. 'No,' he said truthfully. 'You look really nice.'

Vee took off his jacket and perched on his desk, looking very young in his T-shirt. He ran his hands over his hair. 'Look, Kevin, I know what I said was out of order, but I had my reasons. The truth is, I need a favour. You're the only person I can trust.'

'What – me?' Kevin said, astonished. 'But I thought–?'

40

So he likes me after all.

'We're both outsiders,' said Vee in a passionate tone. 'Nothing's ever handed to us on a plate. If we want something, we fight for it, Kevin, don't we? Most people don't understand that.' He fished for his watch with thin electric-looking fingers. 'You're a bright boy, so you've probably guessed that I'm – well – more than human.'

Kevin's mouth fell open.

'I come from another world,' said Vee, looking shy. 'One you've visited, in fact. I come from Afterdark.'

'Oh,' breathed Kevin. 'Like Alice,' he almost whispered.

Vee shifted uncomfortably. 'Oh, yes, Alice,' he said a little wistfully. Then Vee explained that someone, he wouldn't say who, had spread dreadful lies about him. The whole thing was far too painful for Vee to go into now, but the important thing was that it had all ended in a terrible banishing spell.

'I can never go home again. Can you imagine that, Kevin? Believe me, whatever I create in this world for its children to enjoy is only the shadow of a shadow of that enchanted world.'

Kevin closed his eyes. *The shadow of a shadow*, he repeated to himself. Imagine losing a magic kingdom, through no fault of his own. If it was Kevin, he'd want to thump someone for that. He'd demand some serious revenge. But all Vee wanted was to make people happy.

'Couldn't Alice help, you know, clear your name?' Kevin suggested.

Vee glanced at his watch and swallowed hard. 'Kevin, Alice is, let's just say, not my number one fan. She's not very keen on you either, is she?' he added unexpectedly.

Suddenly there were too many Vees in the mirror. All of them watching Kevin.

Kevin scowled at the lilies. 'I couldn't tell you,' he said at last.

'No?' Vee clicked his watch open and shut. 'Has she ever offered to take you into Afterdark, Kevin? No, if I remember rightly, you had to sneak in, like a burglar. But she takes Joe.'

'I don't need a babysitter,' Kevin told the lilies huskily. 'I'm not a little kid.' He blinked to make the flowers stay in focus. He'd never let himself think about how Alice felt about him until now. But, now the hurtful words had been spoken aloud, it seemed to Kevin that Vee must be telling the truth.

'She's taking him again tonight,' Vee said in a casual tone. 'Maybe Joe didn't mention that?'

The lilies were turning into waxy white flames. Kevin wanted to change them back into lilies before he spoke. 'Joe's all right,' he said at last. But his hand clenched itself into a fist.

'You don't need Alice, anyway,' said Vee surprisingly. 'I still have the power to send people into my world, even if I can't go there myself. What do you say to a quest of your own, Kevin? Would you be willing, do you think, to go into my world for me to, er – find something and bring it back here?' Vee made it sound like popping up the road to get a loaf.

Kevin was suddenly suspicious. 'Something like what?'

'Like what, Kevin?' Vee repeated dreamily. 'Like something so precious I'd give everything I own just to hold it in my hands. If you bring it safely back to me,' he added, snapping awake again, 'I promise we'll say no more about the little incident with your brother's jacket. And Jason gets to keep his job. What do you say? Is that a deal?'

Vee smiled warmly right into Kevin's eyes.

And there was another gap in his memories.

When Kevin came back, he was all by himself in Vee's office, staring out over the town, wondering why it was so dark. Then Vermilion clipped in and switched on the light, frightening him to death. 'It's time to go,' she told him in her cool little voice.

Kevin recognised the jacket folded over her arm. 'That's Jay's. How come you've got Jay's jacket?'

Vermilion gave a teeny smile. 'Oh no,' she said. 'This is yours, Kevin. Vee thought you should have your

43

own, now you're working for him. Let's see if I guessed the right size.'

'OK,' said Kevin, with the uneasy feeling that there was something wrong with this gift. *I've been thinking and I can't do that job for Vee after all,* he wanted to say. *I can't go till I've found Archie.* But somehow the words stayed unspoken. He slipped the jacket on and it fitted as though it was made for him.

Then Vermilion was whizzing him breathlessly along empty corridors until they came to a heavy white door. The girl tapped in a musical little code on a row of buttons. 'Quickly,' she said. 'Before we let the heat out.' She opened the door, pulled him through and closed it behind them.

'It's sweltering in here,' said Kevin, surprised. He started to peel off his jacket.

'Leave it,' Vermilion ordered. 'We're not staying.'

It's all right for her, he thought. She's practically in her underwear as it is. But Vermilion was whizzing him along again, between walls of smoky glass.

Years ago, when his grandad was alive, Kevin used to help him in his greenhouse, weeding and pinching out the side-shoots of tomatoes. For some reason this part of Dream Snatchers reminded Kevin of that. Not just the tropical warmth which was making sweat trickle down inside his collar, but the heartbreakingly sweet smell in the air.

'Does Vee collect rare plants? You know, orchids or something?' Kevin asked, puzzled.

'No, not orchids,' said Vermilion, with a private little smile.

'So what's that sweet smell then?' he asked.

Vermilion sighed. 'It's dreams, silly. That's what Vee collects. I thought you'd have guessed by now. That's why it has to be so warm. Otherwise they'd pop off faster than we can catch them. They're right here, behind these walls.'

Kevin touched the glassy surface. 'You mean like a kind of zoo?' he said slowly, trying to understand.

'Yeah,' said Vermilion, as though this idea tickled her. 'A kind of dream zoo.'

'I didn't know.' Kevin's voice was husky with awe. 'I thought dreams were rubbishy films that go on while you're asleep. I didn't know they were alive. Could I, you know, see one?'

'No *way*,' said Vermilion. 'Too many of them die before Vee can use them as it is.'

Kevin had the strangest feeling in the pit of his stomach. 'Use them?' he asked.

'Of course,' said Vermilion. 'You don't think he keeps them for his health, do you?'

'I suppose not,' he whispered.

'What do you think Dream Snatchers runs on, Kevin? Mist?' Vermilion sounded annoyed now.

'Dream Snatchers is a highly complex, extremely time-consuming operation, Kevin. And time is what we're running out of. So hurry!' And, seizing Kevin's hot sweaty hand, she began whizzing him along again through the invisible zoo of dreams.

Then there was a new and worrying gap.

Next time Kevin opened his eyes he was in a hot-air balloon, floating through fog the colour of pond scum. Beside him Vee was complaining about someone. 'She's still such a child,' he was saying. 'Hanging around with those losers, trying to save the world.'

He was talking about Alice, Kevin realised with alarm.

'They'll be storming in any time now,' Vee went on. 'I don't know why they don't give up. Rangers always get scorched to a crisp in the end anyway. They'll never stop me.'

Stop you doing what? Kevin thought, dazed. The fog swirled back and his stomach turned to see the rooftops far below them. And for the first time he realised that Vee's mysterious 'quest' might not be intended to help Vee, so much as to harm Alice and the others.

'Vee,' he said faintly. 'Does Alice want to find that–?'

Vasco wasn't listening. He did something to the

balloon and it began a sharp descent. 'Can you credit it,' he interrupted, pointing down. 'She's actually got a baby with her! It looks like the Mothercare catalogue down there.'

Kevin's eyes pricked with tears when he saw the tiny figures on the roof. I don't want to work for Vee, he thought miserably. I want to be on their side. But it's too late now.

'Oh, here we go,' said Vee wincing. 'Notice that?'

Kevin couldn't hear anything. But he noticed the balloon start to tremble, as if it was being shaken by a rising wind. Then all at once there was a roar and rush of invisible wings and a blast of heat, followed by a surge of perfumed air so sweet and strange, it made Kevin ache with longing. He gazed upwards in awe. The balloon continued to drop steadily through the fog.

Kevin tugged Vee's sleeve. 'How will I know what I'm looking for?' he asked. 'You haven't told me where I've got to go or anything.'

'It'll be obvious when the time comes,' Vee yelled through the racket. 'I've taken care of everything. Trust me.' He grinned his warm affectionate grin.

But Kevin didn't. Not any more. 'How are you, er – sending me?' he shouted.

'I'll whiz you through before Alice closes the door,' said Vee casually. 'While the worlds are still touching.

Stop worrying and leave the details to me.'

So he does need her, thought Kevin. He lied. He lies about everything.

They were heading for Flora's house at sickening speed.

Kevin came to a decision. He began fiddling with the fastenings of his jacket. 'I don't want this any more,' he said.

The balloon dropped abruptly lower, almost grazing a chimney pot.

'Just look at them. This is better than Mary Poppins,' said Vee, amused. Then he looked startled. 'What is the silly girl playing at?'

Kevin's scream stuck in his throat. He couldn't bellow a warning. He couldn't even breathe. He just watched dumb with horror as Joe sailed helplessly out into space. She pushed Joe, he wanted to say. *She pushed him*! The words printed themselves over and over inside his head, but he still wasn't able to understand what he'd seen.

But Joe never hit the ground. With a chime of magic, the fog turned itself inside out like a sock, became a glowing blue tunnel and sucked him in and down like tea-leaves down a drain. When it turned itself right side out again, Joe had vanished.

'That was quite cool,' admitted Vee. 'Cool but annoying. We'll have to rethink our strategy.'

'Oh, no we won't,' said Kevin. He was shaking all over, but somehow he dodged to the opposite side of the balloon and began to scramble out. 'Because I'm going with them.'

He crouched, swaying, on the edge, gathering courage. Only a little way below him now, Alice held out her arms. 'I'll catch you, Kevin,' she called. 'The rangers will be back for us any minute.'

He could see her upturned face, her hair blowing loose. She means it, he thought, his eyes stinging. Alice never lies, never.

'Don't be stupid,' said Vee, grabbing Kevin by his hood. 'We had a deal.'

'I don't care. You called me a thief but you're a worse one. And you're a liar anyway!' Kevin struggled to free himself from Vee's grasp. There was an ugly ripping sound as his hood tore loose. Kevin leaped into Alice's waiting arms. But before he could reach her, something brushed past him – the faintest breath, like a bird fanning its dark wings – and Kevin spun off course, away and down, screaming with terror.

As he went spinning down, he heard Vasco laugh delightedly, as though this was the biggest joke of all.

Then the fog opened for him and Kevin fell through it.

6 The *Rusty Pineapple*

The first things Joe saw in Afterdark were two massive pairs of feet. His eyes travelled disbelievingly upwards.

For a moment it was like a game of statues. The two giants gazing unsmilingly down at Joe and Joe gazing astonished back at them. Then, still without a word, they gently took hold of his elbows with their huge hands and began towing him towards the light.

His companions looked almost severe enough to be angels. But he didn't think even Alice could have organised them. Anyway they didn't have wings, and all those gleaming muscles and fierce tattoos would be quite unexpected in an angel. Besides, angels belonged to the realms of air, and Joe was being drawn silently upward through water, as blue and brilliant as cornflowers. The higher he swam, the happier Joe felt. He still didn't have a clue why Alice pushed him through a hole in the fog, or where precisely in her mysterious kingdom she'd pushed him *to*, but now at least Joe knew she'd delivered him into safe hands. This thought tickled him so much that he broke into a wide underwater grin.

At that moment, without so much as a nod of farewell, the silent giants let him go. As weightless as an angel himself, Joe shot up to the surface. He burst through it with shattering force and came up spluttering in the middle of a tropical ocean. The fret of waves filled the air. A single gull shrieked overhead. For a few seconds, Joe was half-blinded by the glitter of sea and sky. But after a while he made out the shapes of tiny islands, like a bright spill of beads from a broken necklace. The nearest island looked to be within swimming distance.

'So long as there's no sharks,' he said doubtfully.

But just then he noticed a homely flapping sound, like washing in a high wind. Turning his head in surprise, Joe saw a tall wooden ship riding at anchor.

51

The sound came from her tattered, sand-coloured sails as she rose and dipped with the swell. Joe felt a rush of pure delight. Without a second thought, he struck out towards her through the warm blue ocean. He could already hear the rattle of pots and a murmur of voices. From time to time a child coughed.

As he swam closer, Joe saw that the ship was pitted with mysterious scorch marks and, in places, deep blackened scars. A faint reek of burning hung dangerously about her timbers, but Joe scarcely noticed this because of another perfume, so sweet and haunting that his breathing quickened.

He peered up at the battered hulk, trying to make out the faded letters on her prow. 'The *Rusty Pineapple*,' he whispered. A tingle ran through him as if he knew the name of this pirate vessel already and just needed to make sure. Without thinking, Joe reached for a ladder which dangled from the deck. Next minute the rope slithered out of his grasp. How did I know it was there? he thought, astonished. Then he heard a small familiar voice.

'Oooh bite it fishy, bite it.'

'Tat?' said Joe. '*Tat*!' he shouted, delighted.

Someone peered down, pale hair flying across her face like a wing. 'It's Joe,' yelled Flora. 'Come up, Joe! We've been waiting ages.'

As Joe began to haul himself up out of the water,

Flora said hastily, 'I'll get your clothes, shall I?' and vanished again.

Halfway up the ladder, Joe stared at himself in confusion. Someone had fastened an odd shell round his neck. It was shaped a bit like a fish-hook and threaded on a piece of green string. Apart from this, Joe was as naked as the day he was born.

The garments Flora threw at him were soft and faded with salt and sunlight. Joe pulled them on and found they fitted perfectly.

Now I'm really in Afterdark, he told himself. He ducked below decks, happily following the savoury frying smells. Before he reached the galley, Flora appeared and plonked a steaming dish in his hand. 'They say you're to bring your breakfast with you.' She darted ahead of him, down a ribbed passageway, which looked rather like Joe imagined the throat of a whale, and disappeared through a door. Joe followed her into a large room. At the far end was a large table, heaped with charts of some kind. And there, jiggling Flora's baby sister on her knee, and chatting comfortably to a bunch of rough-looking pirates, was Alice, the Princess of Afterdark.

Tat waved a piece of fish at Joe. 'Fish,' she told him, coughing with excitement.

'Good, Joe, you're here,' said the princess as calmly as if he'd wandered in from the next room. 'Spinner

53

was threatening to smash up the furniture if we didn't start in the next five minutes.'

To Joe's amazement, she smiled at the shaggiest, most terrifying-looking pirate of them all. It was Spinner's glittering eyes which scared him. He had bundles of dreadlocked hair like great twisted tree roots.

'You're late, Joe,' said the pirate in a rumbling voice.

'Take no notice,' said someone. 'Spinner's only dangerous until he's eaten everyone else's breakfast as well as his own. Then he's as mild as milk.'

The second pirate looked quite poetic for a pirate, Joe thought. He was bald, but in a slightly noble way, with a beautiful skullcap instead of hair. He was drumming softly on the table, but Joe could tell he didn't really know he was doing it.

'That's Lyle,' whispered Flora. 'The little round one who just came in – he's Floss. He's the cook.'

Spinner broke off a piece of Joe's fish and scoffed it. 'Why don't we let Joe decide who is the more dangerous,' he said with his mouth full. 'A plain speaking, plain dealing man–'

'That's you is it, Spinner?' Lyle interrupted, grinning.

Joe clutched his plate protectively.

'Or,' snarled Spinner, flinging out his arms, 'some baldy in a head-cosy, who thinks truth is beauty and beauty is truth!' He helped himself to one of Joe's

54

strange vegetables. 'That's breadfruit you're scowling at, boy,' he grinned. 'You're in the tropics now.'

Flora was looking scornful. 'You needn't look so scared. Spinner won't hurt you.'

'But what are you all doing on a pirate ship?' Joe hissed back.

Flora's mouth twisted into her knowing little grin. 'They're not pirates – they're rangers,' she began.

This was too much. Joe scraped back his chair. 'Will someone tell me what's going on?' he said loudly. 'I mean – this ship – and that weird perfume. And all of you. It's as if I know it. As if I've been here before. Flora's never even been to Afterdark before, but she acts like she's lived here all her life too. And what's any of it got to do with Vasco Shine?' his voice cracked.

Spinner frowned and reached into his boot. He pulled out an evil-looking knife and jerked his head at the proud-faced old man next to Lyle. 'Tell him, Starbone,' he said. And, with a menacing grin at Joe, he slowly began to carve the peel from an orange.

Starbone pulled down the brim of his black hat, wrapped his blanket closely round him and thought deeply for a moment. 'No,' he said eventually. 'This is a child's story.'

'Which child?' asked Joe desperately. 'Which story?'

'Flora?' said Spinner, looking stern. 'Remember our talk?'

55

Flora wriggled and frowned. 'Do I have to?'

Joe stared at her. 'But why – I mean how–?'

Flora scowled. 'All right, I'll try.' Then she sighed. 'What Spinner wants me to say is that you *have* seen this ship before and so have I. We've seen it in our dreams, loads of times. The difference is, you kind of forget. And the reason I don't, is that my mum – you saw her picture, remember?' Joe nodded dumbly. 'Well, Mum kind of trained me. She came from this world, Joe. From Afterdark. She was a –' Flora took a deep breath as if her next sentence needed all her concentration. But then she looked vague and fiddled with her hair. 'She was a very special person,' she said eventually. 'Alice knew her, didn't you, Alice? I really miss her a lot.' She smiled brightly round the room. 'That's all, really.'

Spinner patted her hand. 'Thank you,' he said. But he looked disappointed, Joe thought.

Alice took over. 'The *Pineapple* is a ranger ship,' she said. 'Every day Spinner and the other rangers here, risk their lives to protect the dream fields, the place your dreams come from, Joe. But Vasco has outwitted us all. That's why we're here. To decide what to do about him.'

'I don't understand,' said Joe. 'Why does Vasco want our dreams anyway? They aren't even real. I know it seems real while you're having one, but afterwards you forget all about it.'

Spinner was looking dangerous again. 'Is that what they teach children in your world?' He thrust his hairy forearms under Joe's nose. 'See these scars?' he growled. 'I got them in the dream fields. Did you notice the burns on the *Pineapple*'s timbers? That's from the toasting we get every time we shift. And that perfume that breaks your heart? Oh, dreams are real, Joe. Terrible, wonderful and absolutely real.'

'Dreams are the stuff you need to *make* things real in the first place,' Lyle explained. 'Without that stuff your world would be a lifeless shadow. No stories, no inventions – no love songs.' Lyle tapped out a complicated rhythm on the sole of his battered boot, grinning to himself. 'Specially no love songs,' he repeated softly.

'And the most magical dream stuff of all is the stuff children's dreams are made of,' said Alice, rocking the sleepy baby in her arms. 'It's purer than gold, deeper than the deepest sea, and wiser than wizards. And it's so powerful. Volcanoes are nothing to it.'

'But it's so new and tender and innocent that Vasco can sweet-talk it into his net before it knows what's happening,' explained Lyle.

'That's how Vasco built Dream Snatchers,' said Spinner. 'With the dream magic he's been stealing from your friends, Joe.'

'And he won't stop there,' said Alice. 'His plans are far grander than that.'

'I *knew* Dream Snatchers was magic,' said Joe, relieved to get something right. 'I just didn't know it was *dream* magic.'

Tat whimpered sleepily and Alice stroked her wispy hair.

'You know Vasco really well, don't you?' said Joe shyly.

'I did once, when we were children,' Alice said. Her eyes were sad. 'But it's too late to save Vasco. The important thing is to stop him.'

'Can we?' asked Joe. From what he'd seen and heard, Vasco Shine was pretty unstoppable.

'We don't know,' said Alice simply.

Spinner tossed away his orange peel. 'You see, up until now, Vasco Shine hasn't exactly stolen dreams, so much as charmed them to him. It's not hard, if you're a vampire. But now Dream Snatchers is ready to open, Vasco is desperate to get at the dream fields themselves.' Spinner sighed. 'He can't go there himself, so he kidnapped your friend.'

'You mean, so Kevin will steal dreams for him? But Kevin would never do that!' Joe said loyally.

'Vasco is terribly dangerous,' said Starbone. 'It's the nature of dream fields to send dreams, just as it's the nature of the sun to spread light and warmth. When children's dreams end up in Vasco's net instead, the fields eagerly send more to replace them. We don't know what the long-term effect of this might be. But if Vasco actually finds a way in –'

'What would he do?' asked Joe, alarmed.

'If he can build himself a shiny palace by charming your dreams into his net,' said Spinner, 'think what he could do if he controlled the source of dreams itself?'

Joe stared at him, feeling slightly sick.

'There might be one way to stop him,' said Alice unexpectedly. 'But it depends on you and Flora.'

Joe's skin began to prickle with magic.

'It may just be a story,' said Floss in a sing-song voice.

'A fairy tale,' growled Spinner.

'But it's our only chance,' whispered Lyle.

'There's a pearl,' Floss told him. 'A pearl that was lost in the deep.'

'Destined to be found by a child from your world,' chanted Starbone.

'The choice is yours,' said Alice, every inch a princess.

There was another silence, so thick with magic, Joe could hardly breathe.

Thanks to Vasco Shine, the magic and the everyday worlds had got dangerously mixed-up with each other. Joe had expected Alice to use her Afterdark influence to put everything right, but she was asking Joe for *his* help. He didn't know if he was proud or terrified.

Joe cleared his throat. 'I'll try,' he said. 'Won't you, Flora?'

Flora looked up. 'Yes, sure,' she said vaguely, as if she'd been thinking about something else.

The rangers sighed with relief. Spinner leaned forward, beaming. But Joe never found out what he was going to say, because outside the porthole a host of sweet voices burst into song.

'*Joke whale joke whale joke whale,*' they sang.

Joe's eyes grew enormous. The *Rusty Pineapple* was in the middle of the ocean. Who could possibly be outside?

Lyle laughed. 'Those girls are such eavesdroppers.'

'It's you they want, Joe,' Spinner grinned.

Joe dashed up on deck, full of curiosity. A crowd of lovely faces shone up at him from the water.

Flora followed. 'They're all boy-mad,' she said sourly. She was in a terrible mood about something. But Joe was thrilled to bits to be meeting real live mermaids.

'Oh – er, hello,' he called down.

At the sound of Joe's voice, the mermaids went wild. '*Joke whale joke whale joke whale,*' they chanted. Some of them whistled piercingly through their fingers. One tossed Joe a garland of tropical blossoms. He put it on bashfully and the mermaids shrieked with excitement.

Flora winced and clutched her ears. 'They might be pretty,' she whispered, 'but they're terribly dim. And their eyes are creepy. Cold and starey, like birds.'

'I think they're sweet.'

The mermaids thought Joe was sweet too. 'We love you, Joke Whale,' cried one, diving beneath a wave with a glitter of her scales.

'Save the children's dreams, Joke,' cried another.

'Find the pearl!' cried a third.

Then the mermaids linked dripping arms round each other's necks and sang a beautiful song which made no sense whatsoever, except for a rather stirring chorus about the heroic Joke Whale and his quest for the Pearl of the Deep. By the fifth chorus Flora's expression was rather glazed. Even Joe thought his face might get stuck in a grateful royal smile for ever.

Then, with a shout of, 'Come and get it, girls!' Floss tipped a bucket out of the galley. Great white lumps sailed through the air. The singers broke off diving in all directions like hungry gulls.

The other rangers came to watch, amused.

'It isn't fish, is it?' asked Joe queasily, as a mermaid caught a lump with a snap of her sharp white teeth.

'Coconut ice,' explained Lyle. 'Mermaids love anything sweet.'

61

'Well, now you've had a hero's send-off,' said Spinner wickedly, 'let's up anchor.'

And the *Rusty Pineapple* turned about, heading for the open sea. The quest for the mysterious Pearl of the Deep had truly begun.

7 The humming-bird room

Kevin sprawled face down, the wind knocked out of him. Somewhere a bird sang its two-note song over and over. Only owls and nightingales sang at night, so probably the bird was a bat. You banged your head too hard, Kevin scolded himself. Bats in the fog? Bats in the belfry, more like.

The landing had jarred him horribly, but nothing

actually seemed to hurt. That could be shock. When Kevin's sister broke her leg she didn't feel a twinge till they lifted her into the ambulance. But it was better not to think about Karen. Funny that it made him feel so homesick, when it was Karen who'd left home, not him.

Kevin sighed. Any minute, he thought, there'd be flashing lights and sirens and kind voices asking him to wriggle his toes. Then maybe he'd let himself remember what happened in the balloon. But for now he'd just lie here in his Dream Snatchers jacket. It was as toasty as a quilt, he thought drowsily, even without the hood. It actually smelled hot, hot and faintly rubbery, like the time Jason tried to mend the telly and it blew up instead . . .

He was on fire! In a flash Kevin was on his feet. 'You *stop* that!' he screamed. He peeled off the smouldering coat, hurling it away from him as hard as he could. It landed too close to the roots of a tropical-looking tree, but he couldn't help that. He'd expected it to crumple in a heap, but the coat billowed uneasily above the ground, glowing fitfully, like a faulty street-lamp. Then tiny tongues of fire sprang out all over it, and, with a great *whuff*, flames leaped up the tree-trunk, sending a gang of tiny birds screeching into the sky. The burning coat turned electric blue, then erupted into witchy little stars, became deathly white and shrivelled into the ground. And then it was over.

If it had been Bonfire Night Kevin might have cheered, but he was dumb with shock. Not a shred of his coat was left. Nothing except a horrible whiff in the air, like a perm his mum once had.

'Oh, boy,' he said, backing away. 'That was nearly me.'

There was a loud splash. Foul-smelling mud squished over the sides of his trainers and splattered up his jeans. Kevin's eyes opened wide. For the first time it struck him as odd that a palm tree had sprouted in Forest Street overnight.

Then he registered that the street itself had vanished. Houses, cars, streetlamp, the lot. Vasco's sly little nudge had been more powerful than Kevin realised. It was too much to take in at once, so he tried to wrestle his trainers out of the thick gluey mud instead. 'Give them back, you,' he panted. 'They cost a fortune.' With disgusting sound effects, the swamp gave in. Kevin fell back in a muddy sprawl and found himself eye to eye with a tiny golden frog. The baby frog pinged high into the air like a golden tiddlywink, and vanished huffily into the swamp.

Kevin gazed at the widening ripples. Palm trees, swamps, frogs. He stared up through tall feathery trees at a sky so blue it took his breath away. He touched his cheek. It felt as warm as a peach in a greenhouse.

'You know what, Dorothy,' he remarked thoughtfully, 'somehow I don't reckon you're in Kansas any more.' Then Kevin's face split into his famous shark's grin and, with a burst of energy, he began to peel off his sweatshirt. 'Oh *boy*!' he said. 'That villain's knocked me clean into Afterdark, that's what he's done!'

All that day, Kevin wandered through landscape so lush and lovely, he kept expecting someone to come crashing after him, to tell him he wasn't allowed. But by and by he began to enjoy himself. This is the place, he thought blissfully.

He couldn't stop touching things. Butterflies. Fallen feathers. Glossy leaves the size of dinner plates. You could *feel* the plants grow here, he thought. He hadn't a clue where in Afterdark 'here' was, and he didn't care. Vasco Shine was a world away. Later on, he might run into the others. Till then, Kevin decided he'd have a nice little holiday. He stuck a purple daisy behind his ear to make it official. He didn't think anyone would miss it. There were flowers everywhere, sneaking their juicy green cables through and over things like mad telephone wires. As for the trees, Kevin had never been impressed with palm trees in pictures, but as he walked under their waving fronds and heard them click in the breeze, like impossibly tall grown-ups gossiping high over his head, he couldn't help smiling. It was like being a little kid, Kevin thought, before he knew summers didn't last and that no Kitchener had come to any good.

It was some time since he'd eaten, so he looked around hopefully for a tree with something familiar growing on it. At last he found one so thick with leaves, that only starbursts of light could get through. Amongst the greenery he vaguely recognised mangoes and pulled one towards him. The fruit plopped into his hand, shaped a bit like a lopsided heart and warm with stored sunlight. He bit into it, spat away the skin and ambled on, munching happily, with juice running down his chin.

After the success of his mango, Kevin got daring and broke open a brittle little fruit like a tiny cup. Inside there was vanilla-flavoured custard, as delicious as any pudding. But the bananas were the real surprise. Fresh, light and slightly honeyed. Nothing like the starchy rubbish his mum bought at the market.

He loped along under the breezy palms, leaving a winding trail of pips and peel.

If it hadn't been for his coat bursting into flames, Kevin might have thought he'd died and gone to heaven.

There was just one thing that bothered him. Every now and then, he thought he heard something following him. *Pad pad pad*, like that. He'd turn sharply and there wouldn't be anything there. He was hearing his own heartbeat or something. And he'd wander on, reassured. Then, after a bit, he'd hear it again. But as soon as Kevin stopped – nothing. It's my trainers, he told himself. That's sad, a bloke spooking himself with his own trainers.

Only it didn't sound like two feet scuffling along the forest floor. It sounded like four.

Then Kevin noticed that the sun was much lower in the sky than it had been. He didn't fancy a night in a tropical forest. Killer spiders and poisonous snakes weren't the half of things that might cosy up to you in the dark. But, to his relief, the trees were already thinning out and the cooling breeze carried a salty tang and the steady sloosh of waves. A beach; now that was more like it. Kevin began to run towards the sound, full of new energy. The sea meant boats, fishermen and maybe a place to sleep.

Then he froze in mid-stride. There it was again. *Pad pad pad*. Only this time the thing didn't stop when Kevin did. It did a bumbling extra pad as if he'd caught it out. Then silence.

'I've had this,' said Kevin fiercely. 'It's been stalking me since I got here.' He clenched his fists. 'All right,' he bellowed. 'Come out, whatever you are. You don't scare me.'

Something scuffled in a bush. Then again, silence.

That's not a person, he thought. It's an animal.

He gulped. The thing was, how big an animal? Lion-sized? But after some thought, Kevin decided he preferred lions, to being on the run from the Thing With No Name.

He spat on the ground for courage. 'Oi – I'm warning you. Come out now or you'll be sorry.' Then, remembering his brief career as a wicked enchanter, he bellowed, 'I – I *summon* you, all right?'

Now, if it was some kind of magic Afterdark beast, it had to show itself, whether it wanted to or not.

But nothing happened.

Then, with a sound like a soft rain shower, all the leaves on the bush shivered at once, showing their pale undersides. The bush began to rock violently as an invisible creature fought its way out. The branches parted with terrible splintering sounds. A mob of little parakeets screamed with alarm.

And out hobbled a hairy little dog.

'*Archie*?' said Kevin, astonished. 'Oh, Archie, how on earth did you get here?'

Tropical sunsets came as a bit of a shock to Kevin. One minute the sky was lit up like a bonfire, the next it was as black as midnight, with stars stuck all over it like pins in a cushion.

Luckily, by then Kevin and Archie had found the shack. It was fairly clean considering, and the fishy smell was bearable with the door propped open. Kevin found no end of handy things when he poked around, including a hurricane lamp and a tinderbox. He lit the lamp at once, to make things more friendly. Then he went scouting for driftwood while Archie sat on the step, sullenly licking his paw.

Minutes later Kevin came pounding back again, dropping wood everywhere. 'Look how much I got,' he said breathlessly. 'That ought to burn all night.'

Archie sighed heavily. There was nothing odd about that. Archie always sighed when humans bored him. Usually Kevin shoved him on to his back and tickled his tummy, to teach him manners. But on a lonely shore, far from his own world, the sound made the tiny hairs stand up on the back of Kevin's neck. He gave an uneasy laugh. 'I could have sworn you were going to talk then.'

He got on with making the fire, setting his little pyramid of kindling as close to the shack as he dared, in case a real lion ambled out of the forest in the night. He struck a spark from the tinderbox. After a few minutes the wood crackled and tiny threads of smoke began to climb into the air.

'Oh, very Robinson Crusoe,' said Kevin proudly.

Then he pulled a deeply unwilling Archie up on his knee and explored his injured paw in the light of the hurricane lamp until he found the thorn that was causing all the trouble.

'Got it,' Kevin told him. 'The bad news is, it looks like Dracula's spare fang, and it's going to hurt. So don't go sinking your vicious little dentures into me again. It's got to be done. All right?'

He gripped Archie in a ferocious neck-lock until the little dog uneasily met his eyes. 'I don't know, Archie,' said Kevin, shaking his head, 'there's something different about you. But I can't put my finger on it.'

There was no doubt about it. Archie wasn't himself. He'd come skulking out of the bush with his hackles up and neck-hairs bristling, almost as if he didn't want Kevin to find him. For a panicky moment Kevin wasn't even sure if this Archie was his Archie, or something only *pretending* to be him. Then, all at once, Archie's little rudder started wagging wildly and the dog came lolloping up on his three good paws and made a huge slobbery fuss of Kevin, like he always did. Kevin sighed with relief and made a big fuss back, only less slobbery. And it was almost all right. Except for when he'd tried to take a look at that fancy silver collar Archie had acquired, and Archie nearly took his hand off.

Archie behaved himself perfectly while Kevin removed the thorn. But the second it was out, the little

71

dog flounced off to a pile of old lobster sacks and turned his back, pointedly licking his wound.

'Be like that,' said Kevin. He blew out the lamp and went to bed.

After his bewildering day Kevin should have dropped off to sleep right away, but he didn't. It was all still swirling round his head like a fairground ride. The zoo of dreams. The balloon. His coat fizzing with stars like a Roman candle.

'I can't blame you for being moody,' he said aloud. 'You didn't ask to be beamed into another world. I'd be cheesed off if it was me. I'm glad we found each other again. I shouted myself hoarse looking for you, Archie Kitchener.'

A bit later Kevin yawned, 'I wish you *could* talk, anyway. Then you could tell me how you got here.' He gazed at the glowing fire and let the soothing sloosh of waves wash over him. His eyelids flickered. 'I wonder what it was?' he murmured. 'That precious whatsit Vee wanted. I'll never know now, eh?' He was just drifting off to sleep when he heard a noise outside and stiffened with fear. It sounded like something crunching bones. Kevin pictured Archie trembling on his lobster sacks in the dark, too scared to bark. Kevin wasn't too happy himself.

'Archie,' he hissed. 'Would you feel any safer if you hopped up here with me? I think I would.'

There were scrabbling noises and a horribly fishy Archie launched himself on to his chest.

'The state of you,' said Kevin fondly. 'Your heart's ticking like a little bomb. Admit it, you were scared, weren't you?'

Archie whined, rolling over to have his tummy tickled.

'That's more like it,' said Kevin. 'I'll look after you and you look after me, eh?' Drowsily wrapping his arms round Archie's warm hairy body, he fell asleep at last.

Clutched to his master's chest, Archie behaved perfectly. He didn't wriggle, scratch his bum or make dreadful smells. He just lay there, softly humming a wordless song, soft as a lullaby, sweet as lemon pie. But never once during the long hours until sunrise, did Archie close his watchful, shining eyes.

Next day Archie's paw was as good as new. And he seemed to have acquired extremely strong opinions about where they should be heading. He trotted bossily down paths, splashed through streams and bounded over rocks, rarely stopping to check that Kevin was following.

You'd think the cocky so-and-so had been here before, thought Kevin. The one time Kevin tried to head in a different direction, Archie set up such a hullabaloo, Kevin decided it was easier to give in than lose an eardrum.

By midday, Kevin longed to rest. But Archie seemed strangely eager to press on. Every so often, he'd slacken the pace long enough to let Kevin gulp down some water, but next minute he went charging off again and Kevin had no choice but to charge after him. He couldn't shake the feeling that Archie knew where he was going. But that was impossible. Then, all at once, he was too shattered to take another step.

'I'm having a breather!' he shouted as Archie went crashing ahead through the bushes. 'Like it or lump it,' he muttered defiantly. He should keep going really. The sun had started its spectacular slide down the sky and they hadn't found anywhere to spend the night.

A sudden thought made Kevin look more closely at the rocks scattered around the place. He ripped away a swathe of passion flower. 'That's not rock,' he said. 'It's an old wall.'

Archie bounded back, yipping impatiently.

'What did your last one die of?' Kevin jeered. 'I'm having a poke around, if it's all the same to your lordship.'

A tiny bat flitted by. Kevin followed its weird antics with uneasy interest. Then he caught sight of something among vivid creepers.

'Say what you like, Archie,' he said slowly, 'but I

74

reckon that's a gatepost. A gatepost with a flying woman on it.'

Archie gave one of his sighs. 'Not a woman as such,' he corrected snootily. 'She's a vampire. Well, you did say I could say what I liked,' he added.

Kevin's eyes widened. He backed away, the colour draining from his face. 'Did you talk? You did, you talked. How did you do that? You never did it before.'

Archie sighed. 'I just thought it would make things easier,' he said. 'Anyway it was you who wished I could, if you remember.'

'When? When did I wish that?'

'When you were falling asleep.'

Kevin was breathing hard. He edged round the little dog, careful to keep his distance. 'Say something else. Something that proves you're my Archie.'

'Like what?' said Archie, vigorously scratching his bottom.

'Like – like – like – what did you drag in through our catflap that made Mum go storming up the wall?'

'That's easy. Next door's Sunday roast, still sizzling and not a slice carved off it. And instead of a pat on the head and a share of the loot, your mother chased me down the street with a squeezy mop. Ask me another.'

Kevin broke into a delighted grin. 'I believe you. Boy, you gave me a fright! I thought something might be sort of *using* you, if you see what I mean. As if you'd let anyone do that!' He rubbed Archie's ears lovingly.

'As if,' said Archie, looking so shocked, Kevin burst out laughing.

'It's funny,' Kevin said. 'I never thought how a talking dog would sound. But you've got such a sweet little voice. I mean, you sound like a dog and everything, but you sound really human too.'

'Thank you,' said Archie coolly, 'but it's going to be dark any minute. Can we continue this talk indoors?' Then, seeing Kevin's baffled expression he said, 'Didn't I mention it? I, er, found a house on the other side of those bushes. It's empty, unless you count the cockroaches and a nest of humming-birds.'

'Archie, you are the coolest dog ever!' Kevin kissed the little dog smack on the nose. Then he began to force his way sturdily through a tangle of morning glory, so he didn't see Archie gaze after him with a wistful expression.

'Did you say "vampire" back there?' Kevin shouted through an unexpected mouthful of blue flowers.

Archie shook himself. 'I did, but maybe the name doesn't have the same sensational meaning here that it does in – in our world.'

'*Oooh*,' Kevin mocked. 'A talking dog *and* a vampire expert. You could go on *Mastermind*.'

'Look, could you concentrate on what you're

doing?' Archie suggested. 'It's not wise to be out of doors when darkness falls. There are – I mean could be – all kinds of unpleasant creatures here. You're lucky you haven't met any already.'

'Oh yeah – creatures like what?'

Archie's lip curled back, showing his teeth. 'Like swamp witches,' he growled. And the hairs stiffened all along his spine.

'And then,' the dog went on edgily, 'there are zombies, otherwise known as the living dead – not to be confused with the *unquiet* dead, which are something else entirely. Shall I go on?'

'No, I get the picture,' shivered Kevin. 'Unsavoury dead geezers: assorted. Let's get indoors.'

And suddenly they were there. Kevin had known to expect a posh house from the fancy gatepost. What he hadn't imagined was its breathtaking loveliness. He followed Archie up the steps of the verandah. 'This is magic,' he breathed.

'Careful,' said Archie. 'The wood's rotten just there.'

'I tell you what though,' said Kevin, shivering again, 'whoever used to live here, they were dead unhappy.'

Archie looked puzzled. 'Why do you say that?'

'I can feel it.' Kevin rubbed his bare arms.

'You could be right,' said Archie strangely. 'Have a look round while I clean this paw. You might find some clothes. You know, boy's clothes which someone left behind,' he added dreamily.

I'll give them a good shake then, Kevin thought. If we're talking cockroaches. But he hankered for clean clothes. So he cautiously opened door after door, whisking dusty sheets off tables with clawed feet and stiff-looking chairs, with a mouse or two nesting in the upholstery, until he found a room which looked as if a boy might once have lived there.

And there was. It was the humming-bird room. Funny, Archie coming to this room straight off, Kevin thought. He peeped at the exquisite little nest, scarcely visible in the confusion of plants which had forced its way in through the windows.

'Don't mind me, birds,' he said softly. The tiny birds gazed at him fearlessly. They'd probably never seen humans before, he thought.

A lizard the size of a hair grip froze on the tiles, its pin-sized eyes bulging.

This must have been a little paradise once, Kevin thought, prising open the rotten slats to let more air in. There was a door leading into the garden. Kevin leaned on it till it juddered open on to a small verandah.

A tangerine tree grew outside, its outline sharp against the darkening sky. The air was full of the scent of blossom. And not just blossom, but a perfume so haunting that Kevin's pulse quickened. It's like that smell at Dream Snatchers, he thought. Only there's much more of it.

There was a little rusting iron bed under the window. At the foot of the bed was a wooden chest, hooped with brass. The chest reminded Kevin too much of one in a film he'd seen with a severed head in it. He lifted the lid with extreme care. There was no horrible, sightless head inside, only books and a bundle of boy's clothes. Archie was right, Kevin thought. On impulse he picked a book off the pile to see who it had belonged to. And had the shock of his life.

For written inside, in a round, childish script, was a name Kevin knew only too well. *Vasco Indigo Shine*.

8 Girls can't fly

Joe slipped into his new sea-going life as easily as if he'd been born to it. When he woke to the creak and dip of the ship and saw another sun-dazzled day flying past his porthole, it was his Afterdark self which felt like the real one, and his old one which seemed a foggy, far-off dream.

Joe still worried though. He worried about Kevin and whether he'd ever see him again. He worried too that their quest might just turn out to be a big wild

80

goose-chase; that Alice and the rangers were pinning their hopes on something which didn't even exist. Because, when he tried asking exactly how some pootling little pearl was meant to stop Vasco Shine using children's dreams to do anything he wanted, no one seemed to know. All anyone could tell him was that once someone, whose name no one remembered, had heard a story which might not be true.

Afterdark is so weird, Joe thought one morning from his favourite perch in the ship's bows. He dangled his feet into the spray, gazing down through clear water at tiny fish flickering silently in and out of the coral. *Imagine people in our world setting off not knowing where they're going or what they'll do when they get there.*

'That's because Afterdarkers trust the magic,' said a voice.

Joe jumped. He wasn't used to people reading his thoughts.

It was Starbone, shivering in his big hat and blanket, despite the heat. 'Magic tells us what we need to know, when the time is right,' he told Joe, with a wintery smile.

'Does it?' Joe asked. 'Does it really?'

'Always,' the old man said stubbornly, and walked away, drawing his blanket round him like a shawl.

Joe gazed after him in astonishment. Then a cool

ripple of sound, like water over pebbles, made him swing his feet back on to the deck. Leaving a trail of damp footprints, he padded off to find Lyle. He knew by now that if Lyle wasn't making music, it was only because he was thinking about music. Even when Lyle was hoisting sails or swabbing the deck, he had some tune or other running through his head and, at the first possible moment, he'd start tapping rhythms on a handy bucket or tabletop. This morning he was twanging the home-made instrument of wood and wire he called a thumb piano. Tat squatted beside him, clapping her small dimpled hands.

'Alice is washing Flora's hair,' Lyle explained. 'So *I'm* the babysitter.'

'Give us a kiss, Titania,' teased Joe. He puckered up his lips. 'Here it comes!'

'Nyeugh!' Tat yelled, scrubbing at her face. 'Stoppit!' Then for the first time she noticed the pale shell hanging round Joe's neck. Her expression changed. 'Mines,' she crooned. 'Oooh pretty mines.' She made a grab for it.

'OK, you have it,' said Joe amiably. Tat became utterly still as he gently retied the piece of thread round her neck.

'Oooh *mines*,' she breathed, as awed as if Joe was giving her diamonds.

Floss and Spinner came to join them. Floss immediately began to produce food from various pockets, like a stage magician. He believed children needed constant feeding.

'Try this.' Floss offered Joe a little purple fruit. 'It's a star apple. The berries are for Flora.'

'Good,' shuddered Joe. The scarlet berries reminded him of something that had been run over.

Spinner pointed through the spray. 'Our friends are back,' he said.

The dolphins had been following them since the first day of the voyage. The rangers said this was because they knew 'the Lady' was with them, meaning Alice. Joe held his breath as the creatures leaped and dived, sometimes grazing the ship with their huge bodies, apparently playing some kind of complicated water dodgems.

'Ever swim with a dolphin?' Floss asked Joe.

'Never,' said Joe, who used to be scared of swimming.

'It's like dipping your head in an underwater library,' said Floss. 'Your head fills up with these huge thoughts. But for all they're so deep, dolphins are just big dogs really. They'll even let you tickle their tummies.'

Tat wriggled a tiny finger. 'Tickle tickle,' she whispered.

Lyle plinked his thumb piano, watching the dolphins through dreamy half-closed eyes.

'So, what's this?' asked Floss, clapping Lyle on the shoulder. 'Not another love song?'

'Of course,' sighed Lyle. 'Love song number 503, I think.'

'Are you in love, Lyle?' asked Joe, amazed.

'Joe's young. He thinks love is for people with hair,' Spinner explained wickedly, shaking his own plentiful locks.

'I don't,' protested Joe.

'Don't let those puppy-dog-eyes fool you, Joe,' Spinner scolded. 'Did Lyle marry his Beauty when he had the chance? Oh, he sang to her in the moonlight about her swan-like neck, dear little toenails and the rest. But then the question of marrying came up and Beauty, being a girl of unusual spirit, as well as having all her own hair—'

'Boil your head, Spinner,' interrupted Lyle calmly.

Tat staggered on to her feet. 'Fishy,' she whispered, her eyes fixed on the dolphins. She twitched her shoulders, frowning.

'Got an itch?' asked Joe. He rubbed her back helpfully. 'Tat, you're burning,' he said, astonished. He drew the little girl gently into the shade.

'Nyeugh!' wailed Tat. 'Stoppit.'

'It's not that I'm bald,' Lyle explained. 'It's just that my hair grows so close to my head.'

Floss gave Tat a piece of banana to distract her.

'Every ranger on this ship has his dreams,' Floss said. 'And you're no different, Spinner. Don't tell me you don't dream of finding those little daughters of yours, one day.'

'Some sorrows are best locked inside a man's heart,' Spinner growled.

It had never occurred to Joe that Spinner had children. Tears sprang to his eyes. Here was this big fiery father without his small daughters and there was Joe Quail without a dad. Sometimes life didn't make sense.

'What are your dreams?' he asked Floss huskily.

Floss was gazing out over the waves. 'I only have one,' he said. 'And it's all down to my grandfather. I was about your age when he told me how he stumbled across a moonhound pup when he was lost near the dream fields one time. The most beautiful beast in creation, it was. Not in its looks, which he said were ungainly, but in its soul. My grandfather couldn't exactly explain what he meant by that. In fact he had to have a measure or two of rum in his belly before he'd speak of it at all. But I know his tale is a true one, because my gran swore my grandfather was a flint-hearted man before that little pup's sweetness rubbed off on him. My gran used to say it was that little pup changed him into a man *worth* marrying.

'I've lived and breathed moonhounds ever since. I

know what they eat, how they raise their young. I've seen dusty bones in museums that *might* be moon-hound bones. I've read learned books about them, listened to storytellers tell drunken tales about them. But never yet have I set eyes on one. But if I could see a moonhound for myself, I know I'd die a better man, like my grandfather before me.'

'You've got loads of time before you die,' said Joe. 'You're really young.'

Floss smiled a little shyly. 'Well, that's my dream. But it's a funny thing about rangers, Joe. Other people's dreams are our life. But we're not always so good at making dreams come true for ourselves.'

Lyle closed his eyes. '*All my life,*' he sang softly, '*I've been chasing after dreams when it seems I should have stayed . . .*' A dolphin did an effortless back flip into the air.

Tat's eyes gleamed. 'Fishy,' she said thickly through her banana.

Floss joined his rough voice to Lyle's. '*I thought I was a winner, I thought I was so wise. Couldn't see that magic often comes disguised . . .*'

Flora came out to dry her hair, saw the berries and began greedily squishing them into her mouth as if she hadn't eaten for days. It was on the tip of Joe's tongue to ask Flora why she only enjoyed disgusting food, but he stopped himself. Things were tense enough between them as it was. Since Joe's first morning on the *Rusty Pineapple*, Flora had avoided him. It wasn't as if Joe was that keen to have her company in the first place, he thought, feeling injured.

The twang of the thumb piano broke into his thoughts. 'Joe must know the chorus by now,' Lyle was saying.

'Even the dolphins know it by now!' said Spinner wearily.

But when the chorus came round again, Spinner joined in with a surprisingly tuneful voice. So did Alice. Even Tat clapped her hands.

'*Maybe you can't catch a dream but you can let your dream catch you,*' carolled Joe.

But Flora just smiled her stiff little smile and flitted silently away.

That night Alice came into Joe's cabin and shook him awake. 'Hurry,' she said urgently.

Joe pulled on his clothes and followed her.

Flora was already up on deck, as pale as a moth in the darkness. Behind her, Lyle was softly unfastening the ropes which secured the little dinghy. They both looked upset.

'What's wrong?' whispered Joe.

'Starbone's fever is worse,' the princess told him. 'He might not live much longer unless he gets the right medicine.'

'What's the matter with him?' Joe asked in alarm.

'Rangers often get this fever, Joe, when they've been working too long in the dream fields and need to go back home for a while. Floss keeps dried herbs in the *Pineapple*'s supplies for this kind of emergency,' Alice went on, 'and I've done what I can with them. But the herb is more powerful if it's freshly picked. Luckily it's quite common on these islands. Flora knows what to look for. I wouldn't ask, Joe, if there was another way.' She hugged him briefly. 'Take care.'

Lyle heaved the dinghy over the side. 'Come on, there's no time to waste.'

First Joe then Flora clambered down the rope ladder and into the tiny boat. Lyle rowed them away from the *Pineapple* with steady strokes.

Joe couldn't bear to think Starbone might die if they didn't bring the herb back in time. 'There isn't even a moon tonight,' he said forlornly.

'Darkness is best where we're going,' said Lyle grimly, as they sped over the water.

Joe felt a twinge of fear.

They crossed the water in silence, broken only by the scream of a night-flying gull, which made Flora flinch and clutch her ears. As they drew closer to the island, the darkness filled with the shrill din of crickets. Joe had already rowed across to the islands with Floss a few times to get supplies and loved every minute of it, but right now all he wanted was to go back to bed. Once he nodded off to sleep, jerking upright to see Flora staring blankly into the night, her face a bleak little moon. Flora never seemed tired, thought Joe. It was one of the many weird things about her.

'After you've gone, I'll row out a little way,' whispered Lyle. 'Otherwise they'll be all over the boat like measles.'

'Who will?' asked Joe, alarmed to hear Lyle planned to stay behind.

Lyle ignored him. 'Head towards the east,' he said. 'It's a small island, so you'll easily find the valley. I'll be waiting.'

Joe climbed out of the boat. A few seconds later, Flora's white face appeared, bobbing beside him in the dark water.

'They may not even notice you,' said Lyle. 'It depends how they feel.'

Joe didn't like the sound of this, but there was no time for questions.

The children splashed ashore and picked their way cautiously up a cliff path in the deep tropical darkness.

'I can't see any lights,' said Joe, peering around. 'Maybe no one lives here after all,' he added hopefully.

'Maybe they don't need light,' snapped Flora. 'Everyone in Afterdark isn't human like you. I'd have thought you'd know that by now.'

Joe wrung sea-water violently from his shirt, wishing it was Flora's neck. Then he remembered Starbone. 'OK, so we're going east,' he said grimly. 'So that's, er–'

'This way,' said Flora. 'East is this way.' And she scrunched away past vague looming shapes which Joe took to be rocks. Joe had noticed Flora's incredible sense of direction before. As if she had a flipping homing device implanted in her brain, he thought bitterly.

Lyle was right. It was only a small island, and after a bit of a climb and rather more of a scramble, they found themselves looking down into a wooded valley, just as night blurred into dawn.

Joe and Flora half-slid down the steep slope. Flora lost her footing and rolled helplessly for the last few metres. Joe ran to help but, to his surprise, she was giggling helplessly. Flora looked almost normal when she laughed, he thought, but it seemed wiser not to say so.

She sat up and looked around her, wonderingly. Then she sniffed the air with its sweet scent of growing things. 'Lemon grass, rose apple, leaf of light, saspodilla.' She flashed Joe a shy smile. 'The leaf of light is the herb we're looking for. My mum was an island girl,' she explained, seeing Joe's surprise. 'Sometimes, when she felt homesick, she used to repeat the names of Afterdark plants to herself. It sounded like a lullaby, the way she said it. Mum was mad about plants.'

'So she knew about herbs as well as dreams?' said Joe curiously. 'She sounds an unusual kind of mum.' He wondered how Flora's parents met, since they came from different worlds, and if this kind of thing was more common than he realised.

Flora's smile vanished as suddenly as it came. 'It'll be light soon,' she snapped. 'Let's get a move on.'

She quickly found the plants they were looking for. There were soft, curiously bright drifts of them growing along the riverbank. The leaf looked as magical as its name, Joe thought.

He could almost have enjoyed the visit to this little secret valley, if he'd been with Kevin instead of this pale prickly girl.

Flora unfastened her shoulder bag and stonily began to fill it with leaves. Joe examined one with interest. It was as green as a lime pickle and so juicy with sap, he was tempted to pop it like seaweed. The truly strange thing about the leaf was that it didn't stop at its edges, but continued for the width of a baby's fingernail, as a shimmer of light. Joe wasn't surprised this herb could make dying men well again. Just one radiant little leaf made him feel as if he could live for ever.

'The flowers are seeding,' he pointed out. 'We could

take some back and plant them in a pot. In case Starbone gets ill again.'

Flora flashed him a surprised look. 'Good idea,' she said grudgingly. 'But we'd better hurry. The sun's almost up.'

They quickly filled the bag and Joe popped in a couple of seeding flower heads. Then they began the climb out of the little valley.

Even though it was uphill now, it seemed to Joe that the return trek took only half as long. In no time they'd be back on board the *Rusty Pineapple* and Starbone could start to get well again.

'This island's really nice,' said Joe cheerfully, scrambling over the rise. 'I don't know what Lyle was on about.'

Then by the pale light of dawn, he saw the path they had taken under cover of darkness.

'Don't you?' said Flora in a scared voice.

They were staring down at the ruins of a small city. Small but extremely creepy. Charred towers rose from the plains like smoke. 'Magicians,' Joe said. 'I bet you horrible magicians used to live in those towers.'

'It looks as if they had a war,' said Flora in her high scared voice.

It's got the same horrible feeling in the air as the valley of the dragons, Joe thought. 'Why didn't we notice it in the dark?' he said aloud.

'I thought they were just rocks,' said Flora unhappily. 'And I was in a hurry to reach the valley.'

'I wasn't *blaming* you,' said Joe. 'Anyway, it looks completely dead from here.'

'That's what I'm scared of,' she whispered.

Joe reached for her hand. 'Ghosts can't hurt you.'

They tramped down the hill hand in hand for comfort. Now it was light, they were forced to notice that they were scrunching through heaps of enchanted-looking ash and possibly even a bone or two.

Suddenly Flora clutched her ears. Then she whirled around. 'They're laughing at me, Joe. They're saying these horrible things. Can't you hear them?'

'Ignore them,' said Joe firmly. 'We'll soon be back at the boat.'

But Flora was panic-stricken. 'Something terrible is going to happen,' she wailed. 'I know it is.' And, to Joe's horror, she dragged her hand out of his and tore off into the ruined city.

Joe stared after her helplessly. Lyle would know what to do, he thought, but fetching him would waste precious time. Flora shouldn't be left here on her own. 'Ghosts can't hurt you, Joe Quail,' he said again, and he scrunched bravely on through the ruins.

The sun was climbing the sky, turning the surrounding hills as blue as heaven. But it didn't feel like heaven. Even the flaunting tropical blossoms seemed sinister now. And there were no birds anywhere, Joe realised.

Where *is* she, he wondered, peering about him. Then he glimpsed the pale wing of Flora's hair flying round the charred stump of a tower and raced after her. 'Flora, wait!' he shouted.

This was Joe's big mistake. His voice bounced from tower to tower, gathering volume, until it sounded like a bellowing crowd of Joes, and still it echoed on and on. 'Flora flora flora. Wait wait wait.' She'll absolutely hate that, he thought, imagining her white-faced, clutching her ears.

Then they came crowding out of the ruins, shadowy figures with eyes as blank as headlamps, all gabbling magic-sounding syllables.

There were sorcerers and witches, djinns and other creatures too strange to think about. Some of the magicians wore jewellery made from things so grue-some, Joe tried hard not to look. Others wielded large bones like clubs.

'I won't disturb you. I just want to find Flora,' he said, swallowing bravely.

But they kept coming, gabbling like turkeys.

On a wild impulse, Joe plunged through them and out the other side. It felt horrible, like an extremely grizzly car-wash, and left him shuddering all over. But the gamble paid off because now he could see Flora's pale skinny limbs flying along ahead of him. Even from here he could see how scared she was.

'Don't run, Flora!' he cried. 'The more scared you get, the more they love it, can't you see?'

The babbling spirits closed in on her in a shadowy swarm. With a squeak of terror, she darted into a ruin and began to climb. Joe could see her perfectly, at every twist of the stairs.

Suddenly Lyle was striding towards him, brushing ghosts aside like mosquitoes. To Joe's amazement, when Lyle saw the frantic little figure flying up the tower with a mob of ghosts in pursuit, he didn't leap to her rescue. Instead he sang out her name, almost as if he was singing love song 503. 'Flora! Get to the top as fast as you can.'

Flora darted a terrified look behind her but did as Lyle said.

'Now what?' said Joe despairingly. 'They'll catch her and kill her.'

Lyle ignored him. 'Brave girl, you're there,' he sang, as her pale hair gleamed out at the top of the tower. 'Now spread your arms wide—'

Flora's scream was blood-curdling. 'No,' she shrieked. 'Don't make me.'

'What?' said Joe. 'What are you making her do?'

'It's the only way,' sang Lyle.

On top of her tower, Flora twisted her hands and moaned.

'You mean – *fly*?' said Joe appalled. 'She's a girl not a bird. She can't.'

Flora moaned again as the first ghosts glimmered into view. Then, to Joe's horror, she actually threw herself clumsily off the tower. She didn't drop like a stone, but nor did she exactly fly. Instead she hovered uneasily in mid-air, like a toy frog on the end of a string.

'I won't,' she was whimpering. 'I just won't.'

Down below her, the ghosts went wild with rage. The ones who had followed her up the tower leaned out and shook their bones at her. The ones on the ground gazed up with empty yellow eyes, fingering their gruesome necklaces, greedily waiting for Flora to fall to her doom.

But Flora didn't. Instead, she fluttered stiffly to a neighbouring tower.

Frothing with fury, the ghosts tore after her.

Flora scowled down from her new perch. 'I won't do this,' she yelled.

'Yes,' sang Lyle sweetly. 'Oh yes, you will. Remember my song? *Magic comes disguised.* You are your mother's beautiful daughter and this is your destiny.'

At Lyle's words, Flora became extremely still. Quite suddenly, she drew herself up to her full height and spread her arms, not stiffly this time, but with style.

Then she soared high over the charred city with its gibbering ghosts, circled it once – a beautiful touch, Joe thought enviously – and headed straight out to sea.

Lyle sighed with relief. 'Let's go. The ghosts will be looking for someone else to feed off now.'

The ranger saw Joe's astonished expression. 'You're right, girls can't fly. But girls who are half-vampire can. Lucky, isn't it?'

9 'Tickle tickle'

'So how come Flora is so chicken about heights?' asked Joe as Lyle rowed away from the island. 'If I could fly I'd do it all the time.'

'Even if everyone thought you were some kind of freak?' said Lyle.

'Yes,' said Joe stoutly. Then he looked ashamed. 'No. Nobody in my class wants to be friends with her, and they don't even know the half – about her being a vampire, I mean.'

'In our world, "vampire" simply means a race of beings with magical powers,' Lyle explained. 'It's only if they don't use those powers wisely that they fall into evil ways.'

'Is that what happened to Vasco?' Joe asked.

But Lyle was still thinking about Flora. 'I'm glad Alice brought her to Afterdark,' he said. 'It will be good for her.'

'She doesn't drink blood, does she?' asked Joe uneasily, remembering Flora's relish for gory-looking food.

'No,' chuckled Lyle. 'Rest easy in your bed, Joe Quail! Flora just needs certain foods to keep her senses sharp.'

'Well it works! She's got ears like a bat – oops,' he clapped his hand to his mouth.

But Lyle was looking thoughtful. 'You did well to stay calm back there. Hungry ghosts feed off the fears of the living. Fear intoxicates them. You did really well,' he repeated so warmly Joe almost burst with pride.

The rangers were delighted when Joe and Lyle arrived back safely. Flora had returned half an hour or so earlier. Even though she was exhausted from her adventures, she'd insisted on helping Alice make a tea from the leaf of light. She'd barely managed to keep her eyes open until Starbone drank it down to the last drop, then she'd dropped into a dead sleep in her chair.

'Spinner carried her to her cabin,' said Floss.

Spinner tried to smile. 'Quite took me back.'

Lyle patted his shoulder. 'You'll have those little girls in your arms again one day.'

Joe crept away, desperate to catch up on his own sleep, but first he peeped in at Starbone. The ranger was awake, propped up on his pillows. Colour was already returning to his face, Joe saw with amazement. 'I brought you the seeds,' he said shyly. 'Did Flora tell you?'

Starbone patted the pouch he wore round his neck. 'They're in here,' he whispered. 'Now get some rest, boy.'

By the time Joe woke again, morning had melted into a golden afternoon. He found Flora up on deck, with her chin on her knees, watching the gulls fighting over scraps. As though she'd been waiting for him, she flipped her hair behind her ears and started talking.

'I wanted to be the same as everyone else,' she explained. 'You can't imagine what it's like to have this spooky secret, that I can't even share with Dad. Oh, he knows Mum was different.' She laughed grimly. 'He just doesn't know how different.'

'She should have told him,' said Joe.

Flora shook her head. 'She knew she could only stay a short time. She said me and Tat were worth it. She said we were special, and one day we'd meet again in her world. I was sort of hoping that when Alice brought me to Afterdark –' Her voice trailed off. 'I never asked to be special,' she burst out suddenly. 'I just want Mum back. I miss her, Joe.'

'I never knew my dad,' said Joe. 'But there's this kind of *nothing* everywhere he's meant to be. Sometimes it feels bigger than the things that really are there, if that doesn't sound stupid.' He touched Flora's hand. 'I'd give anything to do what you did – just step into the air and fly. You should have seen yourself when you got the hang of it, Flora.'

Flora was silent for so long, Joe thought she was crying. 'I thought I must be some kind of monster,' she said at last. 'I was sure you'd hate me, if you knew. Spinner tried to make me tell you. But I couldn't.'

'How did you know about Vee?' Joe asked. 'Do vampires recognise each other or something?'

'It's more a feeling,' said Flora. 'But there are sort of signs. We have bags more energy, for one thing. That's why we don't need so much sleep as you do. Vee half-recognised me too, but he didn't believe it. Vasco Shine's so used to fooling people, it doesn't occur to him he's not the only fake in town.' She grinned.

'But you're so pale, and he's so –'

'Sun-lamp,' said Flora. 'That's my guess, anyway.'

Floss stuck his head out of the galley. 'Hungry, kids?'

'Starving,' Joe yelled back cheerfully. 'But nothing too *red* for me, thanks! Ow, ow!' he yelled as Flora began to pummel him. 'Help! She's killing me. Flora the violent vampire is killing me!'

Everyone was in a party mood that night. Starbone had almost recovered from his mysterious fever. Flora didn't have to pretend not to be a vampire. And everyone told Joe so often that he was a hero, that he began to think there was something in it.

To celebrate, Floss produced·a more than usually fantastic feast. Lyle played and sang, just as if he hadn't been up all night rescuing children from hungry ghosts. Alice sang too, to everyone's delight.

'And by tomorrow the *Rusty Pineapple* will reach the Witches' Kitchen islands,' Spinner said. 'Then the fun really begins!' he added in a mock-sinister voice.

Joe was confident that their quest for the Pearl of the Deep was going to be plain-sailing from now on. He went to bed so happy that when the sun shone in at his porthole the next morning, he was still smiling.

It had been hard for Joe to give up the idea of his own special quest in Afterdark. He'd wanted to outwit villains by himself and take home the pearl in triumph, like the prize at the end of a race. But other people kept getting in the way. Vasco Shine, Flora and her baby sister, even poor Starbone. Now Joe saw that these annoying complications were actually all part of his quest. A quest he was sharing with a bald musician, a cook, a princess and a vampire's daughter.

Then, right in the middle of breakfast, Tat vanished.

It happened under their noses. The children were on deck, eating bread and honey, watching the early morning dolphin display. Tat was so enthralled, she'd been clutching the same crust for ten minutes. 'Tickle tickle,' she murmured to herself.

Spinner prised the wodge out of her hand. 'Let's get you a new piece, sweetheart,' he said. He turned away to cut another slice. Suddenly a dolphin reared up on its tail, uttering birdlike yipping sounds.

'He's calling you, Tat,' Joe joked. He glanced round to see what she made of this new excitement. She'd dropped her mug, he noticed, splashing milk everywhere. He picked it up, looking round for the little girl.

A pair of tiny pale feet with almost transparent toenails floated past his nose.

'Tat!' he mouthed, paralysed with shock.

Spinner turned back with his hands full of bread and realised what was happening. 'Grab her, you idiots!' Both Flora and Joe lunged across the deck.

But Tat was already fluttering gently over the rail. 'Tickle tickle,' she explained, as she flew out over the sparkling blue sea.

The massive body of a dolphin slid between the ship and the flying baby like a cloud and, in less time than it took to blink, Tat was gone and all the dolphins with her.

Spinner and Lyle dived overboard at once. But two hours later there was still no sign of her.

Flora spent the rest of the day sobbing in her cabin.

'She thinks it's her fault,' Floss told Joe. 'You know, for flying. Thinks it must be catching. I told her, it's not like that. There's no telling when a young vampire will get the itch. Tat's got a natural ability for flight, and that's all there is to it.'

Joe thought it was his fault. He'd been there, the first time Tat got that itch. But he hadn't known Flora's sister was a baby vampire then.

That night Alice came to find Joe in his cabin. 'Flora's sleeping,' she said. 'She's cried herself out.'

Joe threw himself into her arms. 'What if we never get Tat back?' he wept. 'What will we do? What will we tell their dad?'

Alice made him look at her. 'Do you trust me to tell the truth, Joe?'

'Yes,' he choked. 'You never lie to me.'

'Then believe me when I say this is for the best.'

'But dolphins can't look after a human baby.'

'Dolphins know more than you think. Tat won't be with them long, in any case. They're taking her to a place where she'll be well looked after.'

Joe wiped his eyes. 'Honestly?'

'Honestly.' Alice met his gaze with her steady grey eyes.

'Have you told Flora?'

'Of course. And I told her the *Pineapple* will sail on to the Witches' Kitchen islands tomorrow as we planned.'

'To look for the pearl?'

'To look for the pearl. Now, sleep. You'll need all your strength for tomorrow.'

'OK,' quavered Joe. As Alice turned to leave, he said, 'Kevin *is* all right, isn't he?'

Alice became very still, as if she was listening to sounds in a distant room. To Joe's alarm, her expression grew troubled. 'Something's wrong,' she said slowly. 'I don't understand how such a thing could happen with the banishment in place, but it has. Kevin reached Afterdark safely, but he didn't come alone.'

'What do you mean?'

'Vasco Shine followed him. Joe, Kevin's in terrible danger.'

10 Finty's infallible skull dazzler

'Vasco Shine,' Kevin said bitterly. 'Vasco blooming Shine. You knew we were coming here. You set me up.' He couldn't bear to look at Archie.

'I didn't mean to,' Archie said very humbly. 'I only did it for your sake. I didn't care what Vasco did to me. But that conniving monster threatened to harm you!' Archie went on like this all day. In fact, by the time Archie finished apologising, Kevin felt quite racked with guilt himself.

That was yesterday.

Now they were on the front verandah, watching the usual spectacular sunset and eating hard-boiled eggs. Kevin had discovered wild chickens roosting in a papaya tree, happy as owls. Their eggs didn't taste weird or anything, but they were extremely small.

'I just remembered,' said Archie brightly, as if the thought just popped into his head. 'I had to show you something. To help you understand Vee.'

'I understand him all right,' said Kevin darkly. 'He's a villain. He's got this zoo full of dreams. Don't know why he wants them. Don't want to neither.'

'Funny, I got the feeling Vee really cared what you thought about him,' said Archie carelessly. 'But then, I'm just a dog.' Archie began to hoover up tiny specks of egg with a tragic expression Kevin recognised only too well.

'Oh, have the rest of mine,' he said wearily. Anything was better than Archie's starving-dog routine. Archie wolfed it dolefully down.

'All right, I give in. What have I got to see?' Kevin sighed.

'When it's dark,' said Archie stubbornly.

So Kevin had to wait until the sun slid behind the coconut palms and the crickets began their metallic night music. Then he followed Archie to Vasco's old room.

'Open the door,' whispered Archie.

Outside the darkness was already as velvety as midnight.

'Climb to the top of the tangerine tree,' said Archie. 'There's lots of toeholds.'

Kevin gave him a hard stare.

'Vee told me,' said Archie hastily. 'You know how he insists on going into every little detail.'

Kevin hoisted himself into the branches. 'That perfume gets strong at night, doesn't it?' he called down. 'I could smell it in my sleep.'

'So could I,' Archie murmured to himself. 'Are you there yet?' he called.

'Yeah, made it!' Kevin yelled. 'Let me get comfy, then you can tell me what I'm looking for.' Then he gasped. 'Oh, Archie.'

'Tell me,' said Archie. There was dreadful longing in his voice. 'Tell me what you see.'

'Fallen stars. Blue fiery fields of them.'

Archie closed his eyes. 'How close are they?' he asked huskily.

'Not very close. Why?'

'Dream fields ebb and flow like the sea. One day they're miles away. Then suddenly they're down the end of your garden. But they always liked this place for some reason. That's why the old Shines built their house here. So they could sit out at nights, enjoying the blue glow, breathing that perfume. Dreams mattered to the Shines in those days.'

'You and Vasco had a nice natter,' Kevin commented. 'Quite a little history lesson.'

'You don't think Vee told me,' said Archie, sounding hurt. 'Dogs read scents the way humans read print. I could tell you the entire history of this house if I liked.'

'This house belonged to vampires, then?' said Kevin, his voice floating down through the dark. 'Those posh Shines that were into dreams and put up fancy gateposts, they were actual vampires?'

'Correct,' said Archie.

'So that makes Vasco Shine one.' Kevin shuddered. 'Should have guessed,' he said bitterly.

'I told you,' sighed Archie. 'It doesn't mean the same here. Besides, he's only half-vampire.'

'Don't tell me, his mummy was a byootiful angel,' teased Kevin.

'She *was* beautiful,' said Archie coldly. 'And unhappy, living so far from her own kind. And almost always ill. His father was away for months at a time. Each time he returned, his mood seemed darker than the time before.'

'Tell me about it,' said Kevin, whose memories of his own dad were not too rosy.

'Of *course* Vee fell in love with dreams,' Archie continued passionately. 'There was nothing else. Nothing.' The dog choked with sobs.

Kevin slithered out of the tree and dragged the miserable Archie on to his lap. 'Forget Vasco. He might have been the Golden Child then, but he's bad news now. Tell me about those fields. Is that where Vee nicks his dreams for Dream Snatchers?'

'If you've got the gift, no actual nicking is involved,' Archie said stiffly. 'It's a question of skill.'

'So Vee inherited this gift from his vampire old man?' Kevin said, trying to get his facts straight.

'Stop wittering about vampires!' shouted Archie. He sprang off Kevin's knee, showing his little jagged teeth. 'Look,' he snarled, 'no one in your world gives a hoot about dreams normally. But run them through some fancy game machine and suddenly people are desperate to pay for them. Vee's just a shrewd, highly successful businessman.'

'No, he's a conniving monster, like *you* said before you joined the Vasco Shine fan club,' said Kevin bitterly.

Archie found a flea under his tail and snapped at it for longer than necessary, in Kevin's opinion. By the time he was facing right way round again, he seemed calmer.

'I'll tell you a story,' he said. 'Before he grew up to

110

be a hideous monster, there was once a small boy called Vasco. He spent his days looking for turtle eggs on the shore, climbing papaya and guava trees, splashing in the warm sea. And sometimes, Kevin, if that boy ran far enough or dived deeply enough, he almost forgot he was lonely.

'But every night the winds from the dream fields blew across his pillow, tugging at his heart with their perfume. Sometimes he imagined they were calling him. But his father had forbidden him to go to the fields or try to look at them, and he daren't disobey.

'One sweet-scented night, Vasco couldn't sleep. He wandered out on to the verandah, rocking himself in the old rocking-chair. Then he couldn't stand it. He had to see. So he climbed up into the tangerine tree. And he saw.'

Kevin closed his eyes dreamily. Suddenly he opened them wide. 'Why do you keep saying, "your world"?'

Archie looked startled. 'I didn't.'

'You did, you said, "No one in your world gives a hoot about dreams",' Kevin quoted.

'Oh, "our world", I meant, of course,' Archie corrected hastily.

'Anyway,' he went on. 'The moment Vasco saw the dream fields he knew they longed for him as much as he longed for them. They belonged together.

'That night, he slept like a baby and, in the

morning, he found their gift for him. A ghostly paw print under his window. The next day there were glimmering tracks, where the creature had prowled around his verandah while Vasco slept. But on the third night, something jumped boldly on to his bed.'

Kevin gasped.

'He was much too scared to look at her,' Archie went on. 'By the time she'd found a comfortable position, she took up nearly all the bed. Slowly the darkness filled with her rich, dangerous purr. And, as if Vasco was her cub, she clamped her paw on his chest, and began licking him with her great rough tongue. It was strangely comforting. By and by the boy fell into a deep sleep. He woke at sunrise, in time to see a leopard bounding back into the fields. After that, the fields sent dream animals to him each night.

'But one night his father came home unexpectedly and saw the glow from the boy's verandah. Next day his father sent for him. He didn't raise his hand or shout. He simply told his son that he was going to send his dream beasts away for ever. And he did.'

Kevin waited for Archie to go on. Instead the little dog's teeth began to chatter. 'Let's go in,' Archie shivered. 'Anyone could be listening.' Kevin suspected Archie was thinking about swamp witches.

Once they were safely behind bolted doors, Archie was his normal cocky self again. 'So we're setting off for the fields tomorrow,' he said breezily.

This was news to Kevin. 'Aren't they dangerous?'

'I've got this hunch your friends will be heading there too,' Archie continued smoothly. 'I thought you'd be keen to join them. If I was wrong–'

'No,' said Kevin, before Archie could sulk again. 'It's a great idea. We'll go.'

That night the scent of dreams wafted through Kevin's window, as haunting as honeysuckle. He hoped they did run into Alice and Joe soon. He was still fond of Archie and everything, but there was something worrying about this new opinionated dachshund. As if he'd acquired an entirely different personality with the gift of human speech.

Just before sunrise, it began to rain. Kevin got out of bed to watch as palm trees darkened in the downpour like sucked pencils. Vivid new grass sprouted before his eyes. Puddles sprang from nowhere, turning into muddy torrents. Archie slumped on the verandah, with his chin on his paws. 'This could go on for days,' he grumbled. 'I should have remembered.'

'Don't be daft,' said Kevin. 'You've never been here before. How could you remember? Don't tell me, you can *smell* it.'

That night, Kevin moved his bed, trying to avoid the drips. The roof leaked like a colander. He positioned pots and pans to catch the worst ones; falling asleep to the uneasy lullaby of raindrops striking metal.

It rained for three days and nights. Then, as if someone had shut off a tap, it stopped. The sun came out. The earth steamed. Humming-birds whirred down to sip from fat scarlet hibiscus blossoms.

'There'll be mud everywhere,' Archie said unhappily, as they finally got ready to leave.

'Don't worry, mate. Any swamp witch has to deal with me first,' Kevin said, grinning his old shark's grin.

Archie stared. For a second Kevin had the eerie sense someone else was looking through Archie's eyes, trying to weigh Kevin up.

Suddenly the little dachshund did a strange thing. Deliberately, almost shyly, he licked Kevin's hand. Then he dashed off madly down the overgrown garden, snarling viciously at a tiny yellow butterfly.

Kevin was quite sad to leave the old house. He gazed back at it for a moment, trying to fix it in his mind, before it disappeared for ever in a jungle of passion flowers and morning glories. Even Archie seemed subdued.

The tide of the dream fields had clearly gone out some way this time, because, hours later, Kevin and his dog were still slogging through mud and the fields were nowhere to be seen.

'By the time we get there, I'm going to have blisters on my blooming blisters,' said Kevin, who had discovered that Vee's old boots were a size too large for him. Secretly Kevin liked wearing Vee's old clothes. He was a real Afterdarker now, with the knife Archie had found him stuck in his belt. Archie had an uncanny instinct for knowing where things were. It was odd how touchy he got if Kevin criticised Vee. As if, deep down, Archie still felt guilty for betraying Kevin to a dream-thief.

'I wonder why *I* don't dream,' Kevin said aloud. 'I dreamed loads when I was little. Must have lost the knack, eh?'

'Dreaming is natural,' said Archie, struggling through the sludge. 'You don't need a knack.' He slithered towards a huge puddle, saving himself in the nick of time by bracing his legs like little hairy skis.

'Natural to a dog, maybe,' said Kevin doubtfully.

Archie's paws skidded from under him again. 'You've got to admit, there's a basic *design* fault here, Kevin,' he wailed, glaring down at his mud-splattered body. 'I mean, am I a dog or a caterpillar, or what?'

'You've always been short and stumpy,' Kevin pointed out. 'Why get in a tizwoz now?'

'Oh, just – just because!' Archie snarled. He floundered through a huge puddle at its deepest point, spraying most of it over Kevin.

Kevin counted slowly to ten. 'Tell you what,' he suggested, more kindly than he felt. 'I'll carry you for a while. Then you walk a bit. And we'll see how we go.'

The landscape grew more rugged. Now and then little brown goats stared suspiciously from the bushes, making Kevin hurry past. Something about their empty yellow eyes gave him the horrors.

Towards the end of the afternoon Archie sniffed the air. 'We've almost caught them up,' he said.

They dragged themselves panting over the hill. And below them, heavily veiled with heat, were the dream fields at last.

What a let-down, thought Kevin in disgust. By daylight, they didn't look anything like as impressive as those starry fields he'd glimpsed from his tangerine tree.

In fact, nothing was how Kevin had pictured it. For a start, he felt there ought to be a wall of some kind, neatly dividing the fields of dreams from the world beyond. And gates, massive ones. And maybe a guard with rippling muscles, like someone on *Gladiators*, with a ferocious sword and a roaring lion or two, for back up.

Instead of these things, there was a small rickety shack. Someone had roofed it with palm fronds, painted it kingfisher blue and nailed a handwritten sign outside. FINTY'S PLACE, it said.

Behind the shack was a flourishing vegetable patch.

Some hens pecked among glossy rows of beans and baby pumpkins. Clearly Finty was no millionaire, but somehow this vivid little shack, planted defiantly in the middle of nowhere, really cheered Kevin up.

'Do you know what this reminds me of?' he said chattily. 'Remember that day Karen and her boyfriend took us to the beach? There was nothing there, was there? Just sea, sand dunes and a hut selling ice-creams. But we all had a dead good time. Don't know why.'

But Archie's lip was drawing back in a snarl. 'Let's get out of here,' he growled. 'Before someone comes.'

He was too late. The door of the shack flew open. A girl in a flaming red dress burst out, aiming an old-fashioned musket at Kevin's boots. 'Go away, you thieving mongoose!' she yelled. 'Or I'll fill your gizzard full of lead!' To show she meant it, she fired the weapon twice, filling the air with gunpowder smells.

Her first shot pinged harmlessly off a bean-pole, but the second struck the rain barrel. Kevin stared at the gushing water in amazement and stuck his hands in the air. 'Blimey,' he said, impressed. 'It's Miss Kitty of Dodge City!'

'Blast,' muttered the girl, reloading furiously. 'First rain for months and I bust up the rain barrel. I'm telling you, boy, get out! I've got nothing here but pumpkins.

I haven't *got* your blasted old pearl and I'm sick of you scoundrels pestering me!'

She's really something, Kevin thought, admiring her swirling red hem and springy curls, all fairly crackling with electricity. So this was Finty.

'I don't know about any pearls,' he told her. 'Honestly.'

The girl lowered her gun warily. 'If you're lying to me, boy –' she began menacingly, then she spotted Archie, backing behind the rain barrel. 'What kind of hound have you got there?'

'A long-haired dachshund,' said Kevin. 'A miniature one.'

Finty spat on the ground. 'Miniature dish mop,' she said scornfully. 'Bewitched more like. What are you doing with an enchanted dog?'

Kevin grinned. 'No, straight up, he's my dog. I've had him since he was a puppy. Archie's just, you know, a dog.'

'Well, I'm telling *you*, the beast's enchanted. It's written all over him like measles.' Finty began polishing her gun with her scarlet hem, flashing her bare ankles. 'You can come in,' she offered. 'If you scrape that mud off your boots. But enchanted beasts stay outside, that's my rule.' She made it sound as if this was a problem which cropped up fairly often.

'I'll just go in for a minute,' he told Archie. He wiped

his boots on a piece of sacking. 'Have you got any scraps I could give my dog?' From where he stood, he could see Archie lapping reproachfully from the leaking barrel. Finty grudgingly gave him some mush she was saving for her hens. 'It's good of her really,' he told Archie. 'Seeing as she thinks you're a demon in disguise.'

But Archie refused to leave the safety of his barrel. 'How can I eat, when you're hobnobbing with *witches*?'

'You've got witches on the brain, you have,' said Kevin despairingly. He went back into Finty's cool dim shack, where she was pouring out some kind of fruit punch for him.

'I ought to dash you under the pump first,' she remarked. 'Looks like you've been through every puddle in Afterdark.'

Kevin took a cautious sip of her punch. It was so delicious, he gulped it thirstily, while she cut him a slice of pumpkin pie. He gazed round curiously. Everything gleamed with cleanliness. As well as being her house, Finty's Place appeared to be a rough and ready kind of bar. Enamel mugs hung from stout hooks and there were rows of bottles with handwritten labels, some with very odd-sounding names. Kevin quite fancied something called *Finty's Infallible Skull Dazzler*. How does she make a living out here? he wondered. Especially if she shoots at all her customers.

'Want your skull dazzled, boy?' Finty grinned, catching him unawares.

Kevin hated to be teased. 'Children don't drink alcohol in my world,' he scowled.

'And they don't run around with enchanted hounds in mine,' she retorted. 'Look, boy, no one comes to Finty's Place without good reason. If you aren't after the pearl, why did you come calling?'

'I didn't mean to come,' said Kevin. 'I was just looking for Alice.'

Finty clapped her hands over her mouth. 'You and she are friends? Oh, I'm mortified! I mean, we were told. We've been waiting. Then you turn up like the story says and I nearly blast your lights out and call you a thieving I-don't-know-what!' She had real tears in her eyes.

'Don't worry,' he said shyly. 'I'm not the boy you're talking about anyway. I'm Kevin. I'm not in anyone's story.'

Finty frowned. 'Isn't yours the world that's plagued by a Shine with its powers all inside out, like ingrown toenails?'

Kevin gave a stunned nod. 'He's stealing our dreams.'

'Then it *is* you that wants the pearl,' declared Finty. 'Well, it'll be a weight off my mind. I mean, it's a *grave* honour and everything, but between you and me, keeping it safe is a damn headache.' She delved in her skirts as if she intended to whip out the mysterious pearl then and there.

'Don't!' said Kevin in a panic. 'Suppose I'm the wrong kid and then the right one turns up tomorrow!'

With a huff of irritation, the girl seized Kevin's hand, tilting it to see his palm. What she saw there made her scowl so horribly that as soon as he had his hand back, Kevin edged closer to the door in case Finty was planning to go for her gun again.

'Did Vasco Shine get those too?' she demanded suddenly.

'Those?' he repeated bewildered.

'Did he get your dreams? There's not one there worth a spit. How can you grow up to be a man without a dream to guide you?'

'Oh, a *plan*, you mean?' said Kevin, grinning with relief. 'For when I grow up and that? Oh, yeah, course I have. Big plans. If they come off,' he boasted, 'I reckon I'll be driving a BMW before I'm thirty.'

Finty tugged so distractedly at her curls, Kevin saw he'd somehow misunderstood. 'Plans can't work without a dream behind them,' she said. 'That would be like planting a pumpkin seed in your shoe. Dreams are like sunlight and rain – oh they're like –'

'It's no use everyone telling me,' Kevin interrupted despairingly. 'I can't dream. I don't know why. Maybe it's because I'm a Kitchener.'

'Why, what's Kitcheners famous for?' Finty frowned.

Kevin was suddenly hot with fury. 'For doing everything WRONG, stupid!' he yelled, jumping to his feet. 'That's the whole point. Kitcheners never do NOTHING right!' His legs were trembling. 'Look, thanks for the sandwich. I'll just get Archie, and we'll go.'

'Go?' repeated Finty looking astonished. 'You can't go yet. A boy who's got himself separated from his dreams, is a mortal danger to himself and others. I couldn't digest my pumpkin pie if I turned you loose like this.'

Her words sent a shiver up Kevin's spine. 'Archie said you're a witch,' he said doubtfully. 'You're not, are you?'

Finty laughed. 'Witch!' she scoffed. 'That's good, from him.' She ran her finger along the bottles, muttering. Finally, she lifted down a small brown bottle with a centimetre or so of liquid left in it and uncorked it.

'Another Finty's infallible,' she told him. She sniffed the bottle with a satisfied expression and fished a battered tin spoon from a jar.

A powerful smell of roses filled the shack, making Kevin oddly light-headed. 'What's that one called?' he asked muzzily.

'I call it, "Kevin Kitchener's Dream",' Finty said with no trace of a smile.

Kevin grinned uneasily. 'But you've only just met me.'

'Dream roses and nothing but dream roses went into this,' the girl told him. 'You're lucky I've got any left. I can only pick them when they grow over my fence. It all depends on the dream tide,' she added mysteriously. She poured out several drops of blood-red liquid. Kevin was alarmed to see them smoke slightly in the spoon.

Then, before he realised what she was doing, Finty pinched his nose, jabbed the spoon between his jaws with her other hand, and from a combination of sheer surprise and helpless fury, he swallowed. He doubled over, fighting for breath, completely incapable of speech. Then a rose-scented burp tore through him and his vision cleared.

'What did you do that for?' he wheezed. 'Thought I was going to light up like a Christmas tree. I haven't even *got* a cough.'

Finty replaced the bottle. 'You'd better go now,' she said. 'You'll want to reach that pearl. Before the opposition gets hold of it,' she added darkly.

'I keep telling you, you're mixing me up with someone else. Anyway, you've got it, haven't you?' said Kevin, now totally confused, as well as reeling from the infallible.

'Mercy, no,' Finty said, delving in her skirt again.

'I've only got the key.' She dropped a rusty little key into Kevin's hand, firmly folding his fingers over it, so that he caught the smell of her skin. She smelled faintly of sunlight, earth and oranges, like his lovely tangerine tree, but with the tiniest hint of gunpowder.

'How did you get it?' he whispered.

Suddenly Finty's eyes seemed very dark. 'The dream fields sent it,' she said softly. 'They send us everything we need, if we'll let them.' Then she flashed her wicked grin. 'Sweet dreams.' And before Kevin could even ask her what her key was the key *to*, Finty shoved him out into the glittering tropical night and shut the door.

'She could have said goodbye,' he muttered. But he couldn't help liking fiery Finty, even if she had tried to poison him. Maybe if he asked her, she'd let him stay a bit. He could weed the garden and learn how to make a skull dazzler. He raised his hand to knock on her bright blue door, then lowered it unhappily.

As he stood there in the darkness, wondering what to do, Kevin had an astonishing thought. That precious thing Vee wanted. It was Finty's pearl, it had to be. And, by amazing coincidence, Kevin had the vital key in his pocket!

'Looks like we're going on that quest after all, Archie,' he said. 'Maybe we'll run into Alice on the way, eh?' He whistled softly. 'Here, boy.' Archie didn't answer. 'Oh, you're not still up for the sulking Olympics?' Kevin thumped the rain barrel. 'Oi! Snap out of it, dog!' But Archie still ignored him.

Suddenly Kevin was seized by a terrible fear. He went down on his knees, groping behind the barrel, and his hands collided with a dish, licked so clean Kevin could see it shining by the light from Finty's window.

Archie had gone.

11 Through the Witches' Kitchen

Joe and Flora were up on deck, playing an Afterdark game, using tiny shells for counters. After Joe won for the second time, Flora said it was too hot to concentrate. They sprawled in the sun, sipping their cool drinks. Floss kept inventing new cocktails for Flora, packed with vampire vitamins. Joe shuddered inwardly each time she swallowed.

126

Flora wanted to hear about Joe's first adventures in Afterdark, so he described them as well as he could. 'I'd love to see my monster again,' he said wistfully. 'Kevin locked him in an underwater dungeon. That was when he was a wicked enchanter,' he explained, seeing Flora's surprise. 'He was sorry later. Anyway, I answered the riddle and set the monster free. It turned out he was the Emperor of Nightfall all the time. He didn't look like an emperor. He had little frondy things on his head, like some old lady's hat. He was having trouble with his feet when I left,' Joe remembered.

'Poor thing, did the dungeon give him chilblains?' asked Flora sympathetically.

'No,' Joe explained. 'He just couldn't decide which sort he liked best!'

Flora spluttered into her ominous crimson drink. Joe had seen Flora's grim little gargoyle smile loads of times. But this was only the second time he'd seen her really laugh.

Suddenly she sniffed the air. 'We're getting near the islands now. I can smell them.'

'Me too.' Joe closed his eyes, inhaling delicious fruit and flower scents, and the smell of coming rain. Then he said, 'Oh!'

For now, mingling with the warm earthy fragrance of the Witches' Kitchen islands was the disturbingly sweet perfume of the dream fields.

After a while, Flora asked thoughtfully, 'How do *you* think we'll find the pearl, Joe?'

Joe didn't need to think. Every night before he went to sleep, he invented brilliant new endings for their quest. 'It's at the bottom of a mysterious lagoon,' he said at once. 'And after we've dived two or three times from a coral reef or something, we spot the wreckage of an ancient ranger ship that went down in a storm hundreds of years ago.'

Joe's favourite part came next. With a crowd of adoring mermaids, he dived to the ocean floor. Shoals of tiny fish escorted him, as he swam silently in through the broken ribs of the ship, his hair floating upwards like weed.

And there, in a chest bursting with pirate gold and precious jewels, was the pearl, as big as an ostrich egg and as creamy pale as the moon.

'So where am I, while this is going on?' Flora asked critically. 'Doing a bit of dusting?'

Joe blushed. 'No, you're there too, stupid,' he said uncomfortably.

'No fear. Not if you're relying on mermaids,' said Flora with her grim little smile. 'If it's not sweets with them, it's jewellery. They'd scratch your eyes out to get that pearl. Mermaids fight really dirty. Nails, teeth, squid ink. You wouldn't believe the things Mum told me. What's a lagoon, anyway?' she asked abruptly.

'It's part of the sea, but a sandbank or something makes it into a lake. Lagoons are calm. And very deep,' Joe hinted.

'Oh,' said Flora, looking less impressed than he'd hoped.

'Well, if our pearl wasn't lost in a wreck, where is it? It's got to be under the sea or else why call it the Pearl of the Deep!'

'Why shouldn't it be deep in the *earth*?' Flora suggested, her eyes sparkling. 'There could be a tiny little island with a smoking volcano on it, and someone really wicked could have thrown the pearl down it, hoping to destroy it for ever. But, just seconds before it plunged down into the molten lava, it landed on a ledge. And it's there, to this day, loyally guarded by tiny salamanders, waiting to be returned to its rightful owner.'

'Guarded by tiny whats?'

'Little creatures that live in fire.'

'Flora Neate, you're a walking Afterdark dictionary,' chortled Floss who had come out for a breath of air. Then he spotted Starbone and the two rangers went off with their heads together, deep in ranger talk.

Joe hated to give up his adoring mermaids, but secretly he was taken with Flora's volcano story. 'How would we get it off that ledge without being barbecued, though?'

Flora was ready for this. 'Probably I'd have to fly down, snatch the pearl and fly back up, before any of the lava splashed on me. We'd have to warn the salamanders, obviously.'

Even though Flora's story starred mainly Flora, Joe was gripped. 'Who do you think threw the pearl in the volcano in the first place?'

'Give me a second and I'll tell you.' Flora hugged her knees while she thought. She was quiet for a surprisingly long time. This had better be good, Joe thought. But for some reason she started shaking her head and whimpering. 'Don't! Don't,' she wailed, in an eerie high-pitched voice. 'Don't hurt him.'

'Flora?' said Joe, feeling a stab of fear. 'Stop messing about.'

But Flora's skin had a greenish tinge. Her terror was real. 'It was his father,' she said in her thin thread of a voice.

'The father said he'd make the dream animals go away for ever. He took him to the swamp witch and left him there all night. She did what the father told her to.' Flora was gasping with distress. 'They took his dreams. They took his dreams,' she moaned. 'They took that little boy's dreams, and the animals didn't know where to find him. He was alone. He was all alone!'

Starbone strode across the deck and seized her

shoulders. 'Don't let it control you!' he ordered, shaking her. 'You don't have to see these things unless you choose.'

Flora snapped awake from her trance. She rubbed her face, with a dazed expression. 'That was horrible,' she said in her normal tone. 'I was making up a story for Joe. Then all of a sudden –' Flora's voice trailed off again, her chin quivering. 'I can't even remember what I said, now,' she wailed.

'You've accepted flight, so other gifts may offer themselves to you,' Starbone explained gently. 'But you don't have to accept them till you're ready.'

'Better come with me and give me a hand in the galley,' said Floss. As he led her away, Floss began to describe in mouthwatering detail, the meal he was planning for that night.

Joe watched them go. What had Flora seen? What did the father do to make the dream animals go away? And who was the small child whose dreams were stolen?

A short time ago, everything had seemed as easy as a children's game of pirate treasure. But all at once the quest for the mysterious pearl had become real. Joe didn't know if he could bear it.

The *Rusty Pineapple* sped on through the waves; her sails swelling and crackling overhead as the warm wind drove her towards the hazy outline of the Witches'

Kitchen islands. The largest island looked like a bowl of spinach, it was so smothered with tropical greenery. Even the pelicans looked glum, bobbing on the waves. Joe hated it. It was too wet, too green and the dismal shore with its grey sand was too creepy for words.

The islands were volcanic, Joe knew, having done zillions of projects on volcanoes. So perhaps he should have been thrilled to see a real one. But the sullen cone-shaped mountain reminded Joe of Flora's terrifying vision. He turned his back on the scenery, pillowed his head on his arms and fell into an uneasy doze.

In his dream, it was darkest midnight and Vasco Shine was chasing them through a tropical forest in his car. Just when they thought they'd got away from him, Vasco leaped out of the trees, wearing a beautiful dinner suit, and grabbed little Tat. He dangled his silver watch in front of them mockingly. 'Dream Snatchers opens tomorrow!' he cried. 'And without the pearl you'll never stop me!'

Joe was shocked awake by a warning clatter of wings. He shot up, his heart racing, to see a pelican hurrying home through a sky golden with sunset. He yawned and rubbed his eyes, registering vaguely that the *Pineapple* had altered course. Then, to his alarm, he saw that the ship was heading rapidly towards a rocky channel between two islands.

It looked an impossibly tight space.

As the tide turned, the water was rushing dramatically into the channel, but found itself trapped and unable to rush out again. The result was a terrifying cauldron, seething and frothing with nightmare force.

'The Witches' Kitchen,' Joe whispered, suddenly understanding. Surely Spinner couldn't be going to risk it, not with darkness coming. 'He'll drown us,' Joe whispered. He wondered if he'd ever see his mum again. This was such a lonely thought that a kind of numbness crept over him. Then above the uproar of the waves he heard someone call his name and suddenly an arm went round him.

'It's all right,' said Alice. 'Spinner knows what he's doing.'

Joe gasped as clouds of spray swept over the deck soaking them both. Needle-sharp rocks towered on either side of them. If Joe reached out, he could almost touch them. He screwed his eyes tightly shut, sure the ship would run aground. But it was worse not knowing, so he forced himself to watch, as inch by painful inch, Spinner coaxed the *Pineapple* between the rocks. Until, just as night fell, she slid smoothly out into open water and a darkness so hushed, Joe could hear himself swallow. Where are we? he thought.

It was like the end of the world. No lights, no sound,

no movement. Nothing but dark and silence.

Then a blue glow appeared on the horizon.

The ship seemed poised, waiting. Alice silently took Joe's hand.

The glow was coming nearer, filling the air with an eerie radiance.

A shiver ran through the ship. An electric excitement, like a surfer getting ready to catch the wave. Joe vaguely heard Spinner bellowing orders. With a deafening roar, the *Pineapple* began to gather speed.

'Look up, Joe,' said Alice, close to his ear.

Joe looked up obediently, as a dazzling wall of blue light rose up and filled the sky, curving to meet them. The ship hurtled recklessly towards it like a comet.

'We're going to collide!' Joe screamed.

'That's the whole point!' the princess yelled back, her hair whipping round her face. Her eyes were shining.

The rush of wind was tremendous, the air full of eerie snatches of sound. The *Rusty Pineapple* groaned as if she might fly apart at the seams. This was the unholy racket he'd heard on the roof, Joe realised. Not dragons after all, but the *Pineapple* herself, her ancient timbers vibrating with effort.

His heart was beating too fast. The sweetness in the air was heart-rending. It was too hot. Joe could hardly breathe. He was going to burn up like a meteorite. He was going to die. He knew he was.

There was an unmistakable jolt as the ship shot through some invisible barrier.

And by degrees the *Pineapple* slowed to her normal cruising speed.

'We're here,' sighed Alice, sounding faintly disappointed. She began briskly combing her hair with her fingers, to get the tangles out.

Ragged cheers and laughter came from various parts of the ship.

But Joe hardly heard. Nothing had prepared him for this. All he could do was stare.

'The dream fields,' he whispered. 'I'm in the actual dream fields.'

Lyle came to gaze over the rail, humming to himself. 'That was a smooth shift,' he said casually. 'Spinner timed that very sweetly.' He yawned as if the effort of shifting had worn him out.

'So what do you think of the fields, Joe, now we've finally caught them up?' Alice asked.

Joe allowed himself to lean against her for a minute. Alice always seemed at home wherever she was. No matter how confusing or frightening life got, Alice was always Alice. A steady star Joe could get his bearings by.

'I love them.'

On the banks of the swiftly flowing river, gauzy

forests, mountains and magical cities came and went like playful dragonflies. Joe stared, enchanted, as a moonlit castle sprouted a little tower as effortlessly as someone growing a fingernail.

'But they're not fields,' he said. 'I mean this is more than *fields*.'

'There are all kinds of fields,' Alice pointed out. 'Fields of poppies, fields of gravity. Force fields. Why not dream fields?'

The tower vanished abruptly and a more elegant one began to form. 'That's better,' said Joe approvingly.

'Not everything that begins here makes an appearance in your world, Joe. But everything in your world once began here,' Lyle explained.

Joe gasped. He'd glimpsed the shapes of beasts prowling along the banks. *Dream animals*, he thought.

Spinner joined them. 'Fun isn't it?' he grinned. 'I love the children's fields. I think that's why I wanted to be a ranger!'

Flora flitted past in a kind of happy trance.

'Did you see the dream animals?' Joe asked her.

She nodded, speechless. Then she clutched his arm. 'Joe – over there! Quickly, quickly!'

And bright as a Polaroid, Joe glimpsed the flash of milky hooves and a blaze of mother of pearl, before the unicorn melted back into the night.

Flora blinked her dazzled eyes. 'Mum always

promised she'd show me one,' she whispered.

'You'll see all sorts here,' said Floss.

Joe had a sudden disturbing thought. 'But you're all up here, with me!' he said, looking around the deck at the assembled crew of the *Pineapple*.

'That's right,' said Lyle cheerfully.

'Then who's sailing the ship?'

Starbone laughed. 'Didn't you feel us shift, Joe?'

'Of course he didn't,' said Spinner with some pride. 'He was in the hands of a master ranger. Smooth as butterscotch, that time.'

'I did feel a tiny jolt,' said Joe, not wanting to sound critical.

'There's always a *bit* of a bump,' Floss agreed. 'But after we shift, the compass is no earthly use anyway, so we let her follow the dream tide.'

Joe stared. 'You mean the ship is sailing *herself*?'

'Things are a bit different in the fields,' said Spinner, grinning.

As the *Rusty Pineapple* sailed on through the dream fields, Flora and Joe darted from one side of the ship to the other, pointing things out.

'I'm sure if I'd been here before, I'd remember,' Joe shouted to Alice.

'You probably haven't,' she told him. 'Children's dreams are mostly sent to them.'

'Postcards from the dream fields,' joked Flora. 'Dear

Joe, wish you were here, try not to forget me, love DF.'

'If Vasco Shine doesn't pinch my mail first,' said Joe.

'If dreamers do visit the dream fields themselves, they usually see through them, anyway,' Alice explained.

'Through them?' Joe echoed, puzzled.

'Well, you wouldn't go to the cinema and waste your ticket watching the projectionist, would you?' said Alice affectionately. 'You're here now as your waking self, Joe. So naturally you want to understand how it all works. But if you were here as the dream-Joe, you'd be so involved in your dream, these thoughts wouldn't even occur to you.' She ruffled his hair. 'Is this making your brain ache?'

He grinned. 'My brain's OK, thanks. So far, anyway.'

Suddenly Flora grabbed his arm again, so desperately Joe yelped with pain. 'What is it now?' he demanded tetchily. '*Two* unicorns?'

Flora was rigid with shock. 'No, it's her! It's my mum!' she whispered.

A pale woman waved excitedly from the bank.

'She's wearing purple,' objected Joe, who had rather fixed ideas about vampire clothing.

Flora's eyes were glued to the woman on the bank. 'Lilac is my mum's favourite colour.'

'Are you sure it's her?' asked Joe. 'I mean, unicorns are one thing, but your mum's actually d –'

'She's my mum, isn't she?' interrupted Flora in a more normal voice. 'Of course I'm sure, bird brain.'

'Go on,' said Alice, giving Flora a little push. 'She's longing to see you. Catch up with us later.'

'What, you mean, *fly* to her?' For a second Flora looked terrified. Then a wicked glint came into her eyes. 'All right, I will then! See you later, alligator!' And Flora sprang joyously into the air. 'Hey, Mum! Look at me!'

Before Flora could reach the riverbank, the woman shook out her pale hair, spread her arms in their floaty lilac sleeves and whooshed dramatically to meet her. 'Fly with me, Flora! Fly with me!'

And Joe was amazed to hear Flora's mum laugh, almost as if she didn't know she was dead, he thought.

Mother and daughter linked hands and soared together into the sky above the dream fields, laughing like loons. Joe gazed after them, wondering what Flora would tell her mum about Tat. He was pleased for Flora and her mum, really, but he couldn't help feeling a bit jealous. But just then, he was astonished to hear someone bellowing at him.

'Oi, Joe Quail! Get them to put the brake on that floating rubbish dump and give us a lift, will you? These boots are killing me!'

On the edge of the dream fields was a sight dearer to Joe than unicorns. A mud-stained boy, sticking out his thumb and grinning a familiar shark's grin.

Then came the strangest thing of all.

'I'm on a quest, Joe,' the boy yelled. 'For some sort of pearl. Does that ring any bells for anyone? Anyway,' he added hoarsely. 'I haven't found it yet. But what I have got, right – is this useful little key! Well, say something, someone,' said Kevin Kitchener.

12 Caught in a dream

'I don't suppose you've seen Archie?' asked Kevin anxiously, as he appeared at the top of the ladder.

'What's he doing here?' said Joe, amazed.

Kevin jumped down on to the deck. 'Good question, Joe,' he sighed. 'But you can bet your life Vasco Shine is mixed up in it somehow.'

Then he caught sight of the princess and his face lit up. 'Oh, cheers, Alice! I met a mate of yours. Girl called Finty. She almost killed me twice,' he added darkly. 'Once with bullets and the second time with some really evil cough medicine! I was hoping to run into you,' he told Joe. 'I've been getting nowhere with this pearl. I wasn't really bothered to start with. Not after that scumbag Vasco tried to trick me into getting it for *him* and everything. But then I thought, "Kevin, Finty must have trusted you to give you that key. You can't let her down." So here I am!'

By the time Kevin stopped for breath, even Alice looked faintly stunned.

'So, what have you been up to, then?' he asked uncomfortably, noticing them all staring.

Just as Joe was going to introduce Kevin, everyone suddenly noticed that an area of the dream fields to Joe's left was growing incredibly full of scenery.

'If it tries to squeeze one more little butterfly in there, it'll blow its buttons off,' muttered Joe.

'That's what it's hoping,' said Kevin, who had apparently seen this happen before.

Joe watched with interest as the landscape grew intensely bright, looking dangerously like a light bulb before it shatters.

'It's getting ready to leave,' Starbone explained.

With a surge of almost irritable energy, the too-bright, too-crowded bit of dream stuff tore itself free. Then, like a whirlwind, it began to swirl itself together, ruthlessly cramming its trees and birds, its stones and

142

stars into a smaller and smaller space.

'It's shrinking itself,' said Joe.

'Wait till you see the next bit,' Kevin told him. 'That's blinding.'

The more it squeezed and squashed itself, the brighter this shrinking dream stuff grew. By this time it was giving off such tremendous heat that Joe and Kevin were shielding their eyes. Then the tiny package of dream stuff exploded into the sky with a burst of perfume so sweet that Joe thought his heart would stop. And it had gone.

'It will pop up in your world now,' said Spinner, making dreams sound as humdrum as toast. 'They cool down by the time they arrive,' he added. 'That's the drawback of this work. You get terrible burns if you're too close when one goes off.'

Joe had never liked to ask about Spinner's mysterious scars.

'Tell you something,' Kevin said, 'it's different when you're down there.'

'Why?' asked Joe.

'Well, up here, it looks pretty. Nice patterns. Wicked special effects. But when you're in the thick of it, you *feel* it. Them fields keep you on your toes,' he warned.

Spinner yawned. 'I don't know about anyone else,' he said rubbing his belly, 'but I'm ready for a snack. What about a picnic up here? If that's OK with our

143

genie of the galley.' He clapped Floss on the shoulder. 'Floss has this hearing problem,' Spinner warned Kevin. 'If someone says "snack" he generally hears "banquet".'

Floss never missed a chance to celebrate. By the time the feast finished arriving, complete with four dazzlingly different puddings, Kevin's eyes were out on stalks.

'He's made four puddings,' he breathed. 'And I'm trying all of them if it kills me.' Then he laughed. 'Death by pudding. Finty never thought of that one, did she!'

By the time they'd eaten most of the picnic, and Kevin was working up to the Finty part of his story, Joe suddenly spotted a tiny figure skimming towards them across the dream fields. He could tell Flora was in a wonderful mood, because instead of flying directly to the *Pineapple*, she was zooming giddily all over the sky. She thinks she's the flipping Red Baron, Joe grinned to himself, remembering how Flora used to be ashamed of her vampire ancestry.

Before Flora Neate arrived in person, Joe had some tricky explaining to do. 'Kevin,' he said. 'There's something you should know about Flora. Something a bit, well – unusual. But if I tell you, you've got to promise not to make any horrible jokes.'

Kevin looked hurt. 'I'd have thought you'd trust me by now, Joe.'

And to Kevin's credit, when Flora finally fluttered down, primly smoothing down her clothes, he didn't blink. 'Cheers, Flora,' he said politely. 'Like your dress.'

Joe was so proud, he could have kissed him.

Then Kevin's face split into his famous evil smirk. 'Well, Bat Girl,' he said chattily, 'I always knew you was *way* above me, know what I mean?' And he howled with laughter at his own wit.

Flora silently began helping herself to pudding. It bothered Joe that he couldn't see her face. If she was going to kill him, he'd rather see it coming. Flora took her bowl over to sit beside Kevin. 'I didn't expect to see you here either, Captain Mud,' she said coolly. 'It's not often us super-heroes meet up.'

'I do look disgusting,' agreed Kevin calmly. 'Course,' he added, 'if I had your bat powers, BG, I could, like, lightly flutter *over* all them puddles.'

Flora giggled, her spoon halfway to her mouth. Then she stopped, glowering. 'You're putting me off my pudding, Joe. Why are you staring?'

'I'm not,' he lied.

To distract her, Joe made Kevin tell his story again for Flora's benefit. When Kevin got to the part where Archie spoke for the first time, Flora was deeply jealous.

'Archie really talked? Out loud? Like we're talking now?'

'Gave me earache some nights,' he said in a weary tone.

'What did he talk *about*?' she asked.

Kevin pondered. 'Well, everything really,' he said at last. 'I'm beginning to think that dog's deeper than I've given him credit for.'

Joe grinned. 'Start your own circus. Kevin Kitchener's Amazing Talking Dog!'

Starbone shook his head. 'The beast is clearly bewitched.'

'Finty kept saying that,' said Kevin anxiously. 'But he's definitely my dog all right. He remembered my mum thundering after him with the mop and everything. He's been a bit moody since he started talking. But he never did me any harm. And now he's lost somewhere. And he's not the bravest dog in the world, Archie isn't.' Kevin swallowed and looked away.

Lyle cleared his throat. 'This Finty,' he said, his voice shaking slightly, '*where* did you say she lived?'

Kevin described the little blue shack, right down to the bottle of skull dazzler.

Lyle jumped up. 'It is her,' he said. 'It's my Finty!' Lyle was so overcome he snatched off his cap and went to stand by the rail, trying to compose himself.

A sudden shiver went through the *Pineapple*.

With dreadful shudderings and creakings, the ship coasted more and more slowly alongside the bank,

146

until at last she came to a standstill.

'What's wrong?' asked Flora in alarm.

'Nothing. Everything's perfect,' said Spinner. 'You've arrived, that's all. Clever girl,' he told the ship.

'Are you sure?' asked Joe doubtfully. 'But how does she know? I mean, she's a lovely ship but she can't think, can she?'

'Now, Joe, you know better than that,' said Floss so reproachfully that Joe flushed scarlet. 'And after she's brought you all this way,' the little cook muttered.

'The *Pineapple* is never wrong,' said Spinner firmly. 'She's saved my neck more than once.'

'We'd come with you, Joe,' Lyle explained, 'but no one over twelve can cross into these fields.'

'You can come, Alice, can't you?' Joe asked hopefully.

Alice shook her head. 'Sorry,' she said sadly. 'I went there all the time when I was a child. But now I have to stay on the ship too.'

'You mean, we've got to go down there on our own? And wander around looking for the pearl? But it could be anywhere!' This place goes on for ever, Joe thought in a panic. And nothing stays the same for more than two seconds. I can't do it. I can't.

But just then Joe felt Starbone's eyes on him. And instead of looking critical of Joe, Starbone's stern old face simply danced with humour. As if he was confident Joe would naturally do the right thing, once he'd calmed down. Joe took a big breath. 'Don't say it,' he sighed. 'I'm meant to trust the magic or something. Is that it?'

'Too right, you are,' Kevin agreed unexpectedly. 'None of us would even be here if it wasn't for magic. You should have seen what happened when Alice threw you off that roof!' he added, grinning.

Joe hadn't known Kevin saw him plummet through the fog. It gave him an odd feeling. But Kevin was right. From the moment the sinister shadow of Vasco's balloon had filled his room, Joe was up to his ears in magic. Why start worrying now? he told himself.

'It's just that sometimes the dream fields seem a bit *too* magic,' he explained.

'Don't forget I can use my super bat powers if things get tough,' Flora teased him. Then her face grew serious again. 'We can't let Vasco win, Joe.'

Alice gave him one of her quick hugs.

'Well, let's get on with it,' said Kevin.

One by one the three children said their goodbyes and jumped down on to the dream fields. Joe went last of all, feeling as jittery as if he was about to set foot on a new planet. 'It isn't squishy, is it?' he called down.

Flora gave a startled squeak. 'No, but it feels like pins and needles.'

By then, Joe had joined her on the tingling earth. And the moment he was inside them, the dragonfly gauziness of the dream fields was ripped away like a blue veil. Brilliant colours, sweet scents and sounds and delicious feelings jumped out at him in a great shout of joy. It was almost too much to bear. For everything in the dream fields was not just bigger and brighter, but ten times as *alive* as the waking world.

Then he made the mistake of glancing back at the *Pineapple*.

The ship had vanished. More alarmingly, so had the river. There were only the dream fields, endlessly filling and emptying, like a beautiful tide.

'It's all right,' Flora reassured him. 'Everyone's still there. You just can't see them. I should have warned you. It really tested my radar, finding my way back to the ship.'

'But why can't we see the river?' asked Joe.

'Because the river isn't part of the dream, it's just the way in. And in the fields, the only real thing is the dream,' Flora explained.

'Are you saying we were invisible too? Sailing invisibly down an invisible river on an invisible ship.'

Flora nodded.

'That's rubbish. How did Kevin see us then?'

'Because we're part of Kevin's dream and he's part of ours. We had to meet up, don't you see? So we could find the pearl.'

'Don't think about it, Joe,' Kevin warned. 'It'll only do your head in.' He began to lope ahead, shouting over his shoulder. 'The fields don't have exactly the same rules as back home. But you start noticing helpful little signs.'

'Signs,' said Joe blankly. 'What kind of signs?'

'I know what he means,' said Flora. 'You have to find the one thing that doesn't change and follow it, like a thread. It could be anything. A colour or a scent. Just so long as it belongs to your dream.'

'And how are you meant to know that?' asked Joe grumpily.

Flora tapped her chest. 'You feel it.'

'See, we'll all go nuts, Joe, if we rely on trees for landmarks and that,' said Kevin. 'Because, before you know it, your dream tree's turned into a blooming spaceship or something, and then where are you? Flaming Norah, what did I tell you!'

Kevin sprang back in alarm as the air filled with a thundering sound. The ground began to tremble. But instead of the earth cracking open at their feet, the children found themselves staring up at a gigantic waterfall, apparently tumbling down through a hole in the sky.

'Now that really does your head in,' said Kevin in awe.

Without visible support of any kind, the waterfall cascaded from level to level, like a dazzling watery stair, finally vanishing into the earth without leaving a drop of moisture behind.

It was the most astonishing thing Joe had seen.

'Pure as gold, deep as the deepest sea and wiser than wizards,' he murmured.

'Come again?' asked Kevin, suspicious of anything that sounded like poetry.

Joe repeated it awkwardly. 'I didn't make it up. It's what Alice said about dreams.'

Flora stopped in her tracks. 'Deep as the deepest sea,' she repeated. Then her eyes opened wide. 'Joe, think about it. That's where the pearl was lost. Not under the sea or inside the earth. But in a dream. A deep, deep dream. The most secret place anyone could ever hide something.'

'Yeah?' said Kevin sceptically. 'You don't think this is all just a bit *too* deep, do you?'

'So a child must have –' Joe began to say. But then he forgot what he'd been going to say, because a leopard strolled out of the dream fields, half as big again as the waking kind and so burningly beautiful it hurt to look at it.

It never occurred to Joe that the beast might harm

151

them. But Kevin went white, then he stuttered with excitement, 'It's a sign. Like I was saying. Remember? A sign that belongs to your dream? Well, this is mine, Joe. This is my sign!'

The dream leopard rasped her tongue down her chest, ambled a few paces and glanced back.

'She wants us to follow her!' hissed Kevin. 'She'll lead us to the pearl. I know she will.'

'Not until you tell us *why* that leopard is a sign,' demanded Flora.

The leopard padded on for a few more steps, turned to see if the children were following, then sprang away impatiently into the bushes.

'There's no time. Just trust me,' cried Kevin desperately. 'Even if you never trust me again, trust me now!' And he tore away after the dream leopard.

Joe and Flora exchanged looks.

'Well, he's your friend,' said Flora fiercely. 'If you don't trust him, who will? Come on, before we lose him!'

At first, it was bewildering, running through the fields as dreams flickered in and out of view.

Then gradually Joe saw how it worked. If he kept his attention on the leopard long enough, she responded, by growing larger, brighter and more golden. And suddenly it was obvious that everything else around her was purely scenery. Other people's dream scenery, with no business in Joe's dream. The leopard bounded on ahead, drawing the children with her, as surely as if a thread connected them. The invisible thread of the dream.

They followed the leopard through a rapid succession of climates and seasons, through day and night. They splashed after her through a shallow sea of lilies. They ran across rooftops, through fog haunted by the sinister shadows of balloons. Once, as they chased the leopard through a deserted glass city, a pearly car came hurtling out of the dark and they veered round it and kept on running. But they were still only touching the outer edges of the dream. So they ran harder and faster.

The leopard led them into a ruined palace, with giant steps higher than Joe's waist. And at the top of the steps, they found it waiting in a dappled golden sprawl. Then the leopard poured itself over a rocky ledge and they sprang down after it into a narrow street, lively with jugglers, fire-eaters and acrobats. Abruptly, the dream leopard dived through a doorway and so did the children. But instead of crashing through someone's living-room, Joe found himself running across a green plain, in front of a herd of stampeding horses. The dream horses melted through him as softly as snowflakes and thundered on. And when he dared to open his eyes again, the leopard was bounding ahead under a starry night sky, leading them deeper into the dream.

The tingling in Joe's feet was unbearable. We're almost there, he thought, wild with excitement. Like a song on an old gramophone, the fast-flowing scenery ran more slowly. The landscape began to simplify. Their surroundings grew brighter, larger and increasingly solid. Until there was only one dream. This one. A warm moist breeze blew across Joe's skin. A soft, almost tender light drenched everything.

The three children were walking under papaya trees, towards a pair of iron gates with ornamental gateposts on either side. On each one, Joe noticed, there was a stone woman in a flying pose.

Flora peered at them curiously. 'Say what you like, but those are vampires.'

And suddenly Kevin turned white and slumped to the ground with his head in his hands. No longer needing to look back, the leopard nudged its way through the gates, sprang through lemon grass, over hibiscus and under morning glories, trotted up the steps of a verandah and vanished into a house. But, by then, Vasco Shine's dream had already tightened round them like a spell. And they were trapped.

13 The Pearl of the Deep

Kevin wouldn't budge. 'I'm telling you,' he said hopelessly, 'you can forget about this quest. We're done for. This isn't our dream. It's *his*.'

'Are you absolutely sure this is his house?' asked Flora.

Through his blur of terror, Joe noticed that Flora hardly seemed scared at all. She almost sounded excited.

'I stayed in Vasco's real house, didn't I?' wailed

Kevin. 'I slept in his little childhood bed and borrowed his clothes and everything. You can't exactly forget a vampire gatepost now, can you?' He smashed his fist into the iron gate, with its ominous stars and moons.

'You never said that was Vasco's house,' said Joe, completely thunderstruck.

'You don't think I wanted to go?' said Kevin. 'Archie tricked me so I'd get the pearl for Vasco. I was gutted when I found out.' He saw the look on Joe's face. 'That's why I didn't tell you. I knew you'd think I was working for the scumbag too.'

'Well, if you're going to sit here feeling sorry for yourselves while Vasco turns our world into one big Dream Snatchers,' said Flora in disgust, 'I'll go and get the pearl myself.' And she stormed through the gate and into the light-drenched garden. Kevin and Joe jumped up and ran after her.

'You don't seriously think the pearl's in there?' hissed Kevin. 'I'll tell you what's in there, old Vasco, waiting to clobber us.'

'So, Kevin, why did we have to follow that leopard, again, I can't remember?' said Flora sarcastically.

'But that was before I knew it was a trick, not a sign!' wailed Kevin.

'Look, either something's a sign or it isn't,' she yelled. 'If it's a sign, you follow it until you get where you're going. You don't give up because things work out differently to what you thought, and whine about being tricked.'

Flora's stomping steps had brought them all to the verandah.

'Well, you can talk,' said Joe, equally furious. 'I know you're a born-again vampire now, but you weren't so brave yourself when you first got to Afterdark!'

There was a tense silence. After a while, Flora cleared her throat. Joe looked up warily and saw she was almost in tears.

'I'm sorry. I know I'm not very good at everyday life, Joe, but I am half-vampire so I really do know about dreams. You mustn't be put off so easily, Kevin,' she said, her voice squeaking with distress. 'You'll never get anywhere like that. In dreams you've got to go by signs and feelings.'

'Feelings?' said Kevin, looking blank. 'You've totally lost me now.'

Flora gestured at the lovely low house in its lush garden. 'How does this dream feel? Does this honestly feel like the kind of thing Vasco would dream now?'

'No,' admitted Kevin. 'His one would be full of cool cars and girls and being on chat shows in a suit.'

'But if it's not Vasco's,' asked Joe puzzled, 'whose dream is it?'

'Oh, it is Vasco's. Just not *now*.' Flora skipped breezily up the steps and into the house.

Kevin's lips quivered with the beginnings of his famous smirk. 'Vampire girls,' he whispered wickedly. 'Can't live with them. Can't live without them.'

Then Joe understood.

It isn't Vasco's dream as he is now, he thought, because it's *then*. When Vasco was a child.

And he followed Flora into the house.

Flora narrowed her eyes. 'There's something very odd about all this light,' she said. 'I can't think what it is.'

'No shadows,' said Kevin suddenly. 'Weird.'

'Maybe Flora's right. Maybe the pearl is here after all,' said Joe. The light could be coming from that, he thought, with a little rush of hope.

A tiny feather dropped at their feet and drifted briefly across the tiles. Kevin bent to pick it up. 'That's a humming-bird feather, that is.' His anxious face brightened.

'No,' said Flora triumphantly. 'It's another sign, that is. Come on.'

Joe and Kevin followed her into another light-drenched room. It was full of grand furniture. In Joe's opinion, it was a bit too full.

'All the old vampire aristocracy went in for this fancy stuff,' said Flora shuddering. 'I can't stand it. All those horrible carved twiddly bits and tables with claws.'

Kevin was staring up at a large painting. 'That must be them. Mr and Mrs Vampire-Shine.'

Vasco's handsome father looked uncannily like his dream-snatching son. But there was something in his eyes which made Joe's skin creep.

'I don't fancy the look of him, do you?' Kevin shivered. 'No offence, Flora, but he looks a right old vampire. Vee's mum's all right though. Archie said she was pretty.'

'*She's* not a vampire,' mused Flora, staring critically at the painting. 'I wonder what she is. They can't have been happy. He's got too much darkness in him and if you ask me, she hasn't got nearly enough. I bet she hated his furniture, don't you?'

Then she gave Kevin a startled look. 'How did Archie know about Vasco's mum?' she asked.

'Oh, it's some dog thing,' he said carelessly. 'They pick up history from smells and stuff.'

The children continued exploring. Apart from the surplus light and lack of shadow, the only obviously dreamlike thing about the house was that, as they went from room to room, other tiny objects occasionally appeared out of the air. Once it was a shell and after that a bright button, and then a toy made out of a tin.

'Some kid's made that,' said Kevin, examining the toy. 'I bet it took him hours.'

Flora held out her hand for it. 'I'll keep this one for Tat.'

Soon they had quite a collection of bits and bobs. Much like the sort of stuff Joe kept in his pockets when he was very small.

It was all very strange.

'It's a trail,' Flora said suddenly, 'like Hansel and Gretel's pebbles.'

Joe's eyes lit up. 'A trail to the pearl!'

At almost the same moment Kevin said, 'I'm stupid. We should have gone straight to his room. That's where it'll be, if it's anywhere.'

They were rewarded by a golden glimpse, as the leopard disappeared down a corridor.

'That's a sign,' sang Flora and Kevin together, and the children raced after the leopard. When they reached the door of Vasco Shine's room, she was waiting for them.

'You need a bit of a knack for this door,' said Kevin.

'Get on with it, then,' said Flora.

As he waited impatiently for Kevin to juggle the temperamental handle, Joe's heart bumped with a kind of painful joy. It's here, he thought. We've nearly found the pearl! And Joe was suddenly sure that the light was stronger outside this room than anywhere else in the house.

Kevin gave an extra lunge and at last the door opened.

'Flaming Norah,' said Kevin.

They stared. Behind the door there was another door.

'What do you bet that's a two-way mirror up there and old Vasco's watching us, laughing his designer socks off?' said Kevin despairingly.

'Don't get into a froth,' snapped Flora. 'Open that one too.'

Joe tried the handle. 'No, this one's actually locked,' he said puzzled. 'Didn't Finty give you a key?' he asked Kevin.

'Yeah. But I never thought it belonged to some scumbag's bedroom door. I was more thinking like treasure chests.'

'Maybe you'll find the treasure chest inside,' suggested Joe.

'And then again, maybe it'll be Bluebeard's gruesome chamber,' said Kevin darkly. He felt around anxiously in his pockets. 'Someone tell me how a real key with real rust on it can actually open a dream door,' he jeered.

But Joe was watching as Kevin fitted the key to the lock, so he saw how much his hand shook.

Flora giggled with nerves. 'Don't think about it, Kevin. It'll do your head in.'

The key turned easily. Before Kevin could get the door properly open, the leopard nudged through it and into the room beyond. And on the other side of the door, it was dark. Midnight darkness, splashed with brilliant stars and full of sweet scents, sounds and dangerous, flitting shadows.

Joe glanced back in bewilderment. Behind him, the other rooms still shone with their unchanging summer light. It was like a child's picture book, showing the difference between day and night.

'In my one,' Kevin pointed out huskily, 'the tree was outside and all the furniture was indoors.'

'This is indoors,' said Flora, her eyes glinting with pleasure. 'When you're a vampire, night is your room.'

'It's indoors and outdoors,' said Joe. 'So you're both right.' That's what made it so mysterious. At one and the same time, this was both a child's homely little room and the glittering limitless night. Then Joe noticed the leopard staring at him, her tail switching to and fro. Her eyes were a blaze of longing. 'What do you want?' he asked gently, as if she was a cat he'd met in the street. 'Come on, show me!'

As if Joe's question had unlocked a final mystery, a small iron bed appeared, floating on the darkness. A flickering light surrounded it, like the soft glow of a child's night-light. The leopard launched herself into the darkness, making her way towards the bed with a

162

dreamlike motion which was part-swimming, part-flight.

'She wants us to follow her,' said Kevin.

Never taking their eyes off the dream leopard, the children too half-swam, half-flew through a rich, fathomless darkness which had no walls, floors or boundaries of any kind. The leopard leaped up on to the bed, curling herself jealously around something.

'Is it cubs?' asked Joe.

'It's the pearl, isn't it?' asked Flora eagerly.

'You won't believe this,' said Kevin, who had a better view. 'But actually it's some kid.'

Joe used the bedpost to hoist himself up, and saw a dark-haired boy of perhaps five years old nestling against the dappled coat of the leopard. He was sleeping deeply, his small hands loosely curled. And Joe could see he had a startling resemblance to Vasco Shine.

'So that's our little dreamer,' said Flora softly. The boy's eyelids quivered, as if he was listening to them inside his dream.

'You mean, we're in his dream,' breathed Joe. 'But why would some little boy want to catch us in his dream?'

'Because of Vasco's father stealing him from Vasco,' she said. 'He wants to put it right.'

Joe realised Flora was talking about her terrifying vision. 'You mean that little kid you saw was *Vasco*?'

Yet it was obvious. The most obvious thing in the world.

'It's not some weird vampire thing. We're all born with a dream self inside us,' Flora explained. 'But when Vasco was small, his father used some disgusting kind of swamp magic to separate him from his. Then he took Vasco's dream self and hid him where he knew Vasco couldn't reach him in a million years. Inside his own dreams. Quite clever, really,' she said, looking slightly sick.

Kevin was having trouble breathing. 'That's – that's well out of order, that is!' he cried at last. 'His old man couldn't go tampering like that! I mean, this place belongs to children. Not even the rangers, not even *Alice* is allowed in here!'

'He did it all the same,' said Flora quietly.

Kevin looked despairing. 'So this little tyke is in here with all the lovely dreams. And scumbag's out there with the evil schemes. It's a mess this, isn't it?'

While they were talking, Joe was vaguely aware of an object lying half under the child's pillow. It glinted silver in the night-light glow. Suddenly he noticed a faint ticking sound.

'That's Vasco's watch,' he said, astonished. 'What's it doing here?'

Flora climbed up on to the bed. The leopard began

to purr with a sound as rich and dangerous as the night itself.

'Come up here and I'll tell you,' Flora said, patting the covers.

'Won't we wake him?' asked Kevin.

Flora shook her head. 'He is awake actually, inside his dreams. It's a different sort of awake to ours, that's all. But he knows everything that's going on, Kevin. Better than Vasco does anyway,' she sighed. They scrambled up beside her.

'You know that vision?' she said to Joe. 'Well, it didn't stop after I went off with Floss. I kept getting flashes for the rest of the day. I'd hear this little boy screaming. Then I'd see a watch, shining and ticking and shining. As if someone was showing it to him, to make him stop crying.'

'Of course he screamed,' said Kevin looking sick himself. 'I mean, after Vee's dad did – you know. His dream animals couldn't come round to play no more, could they? I'd scream – wouldn't you? And then they go, "never mind your silly dreams, darling, have this nice watch!"'

'I think Vasco was ill afterwards,' said Flora. 'And when he was well again, his dad gave him the watch to keep.'

'When he was *well*,' said Joe disgustedly. 'How could he be well?'

'Have you noticed how everything comes in twos with Vasco?' said Kevin wearily. 'Two kids, two worlds, two watches. Double trouble he's been from start to finish.'

'That's why we're here,' said Flora. 'I think.'

'You know he's lying here, dreaming his little socks off and that?' Kevin said suddenly. Joe and Flora nodded. 'Well, Vasco's not getting them, is he? So where do they *go*?'

Now Kevin had asked it, this was such an obvious question that Joe and Flora stared at him, electrified. But before they could answer, the leopard yawned and casually flung out a lazy paw, knocking the child's hand. The small fingers of the sleeping boy uncurled. On his open palm was a dark glistening pearl. There was a stunned silence.

Flora whispered, 'We never imagined this, Joe.'

'They go in there,' he breathed.

Flora scrubbed her hand across her face. 'He's taken care of them all these years,' she said. 'I think that's why the dream fields helped him.'

Joe gazed at her. 'The dream fields?' he repeated slowly. It was the dream fields which had brought them to this room full of night. The dream fields which whispered a story of a mysterious pearl to whoever could hear it; so children from another world would one day set off on a terrifying quest. And to help them find their way, it kept up a stream of signs and wonders: unicorns, rusty keys and humming-bird feathers.

'So we've got to give the pearl to Vasco, then?' Joe said uncertainly.

'Don't be stupid,' said Kevin. 'How Vee is now, he'd just say, "Oh ta very much, kids," and use it to build a chain of Dream Snatchers. No, Joe, it's got to be Alice. She'll know what to do with it. I'll take it, shall I?' he asked abruptly. There was something so desperate in his face that Joe and Flora just nodded silently.

So Kevin took the pearl carefully from the small trusting palm. At his touch, the floating bed with its sleeping child, its leopard guardian and the mysterious room filled with night, all dissolved. And they were in the dream fields, a few metres from a river. Bobbing in front of them was a familiar ship, her sand-coloured sails flapping like washing in a high wind. Busy scrubbing sounds came from somewhere and the sound of Lyle trying out his latest song.

Kevin's forehead crumpled into a baffled scowl. 'So where have we been, then? Where the blazes have we been all this time?' In a sudden panic, he opened his hand. But the pearl was still there.

Alice waved to them from the deck.

'Shall we tell them?' Joe whispered.

'Let's make them suffer a bit,' grinned Kevin.

Then Joe heard a noise. Like the sound a small

animal might make, padding through leaves.

Kevin's eyes grew soft with delight. 'I don't believe it,' he cried. 'Happy endings all round. It's my Archie! Here, boy,' he called. 'You're just in time to get a lift home with your dad.' He squatted down, calling and coaxing. At last a small bedraggled dog shot out of the bushes.

'Oh, he is so sweet,' cried Flora.

But Alice cried anxiously, 'Don't let him touch you, Kevin!'

The dog sprang at Kevin growling. Kevin dived out of the way, but somehow Archie's collar knocked painfully against the knuckles of the hand which held the pearl. Kevin staggered back, sucking his fist, bewildered. There was a jagged spurt of blue fire. Archie's short legs sagged from under him and he crumpled on his side, staring emptily at the sky.

'I think you've got something for me,' said a warm light voice. 'Wasn't that our deal, Kevin?'

And beside Kevin, in his perfect clothes, was Vasco Shine.

Kevin looked helplessly from Vasco to his dead dog and back again. He began to shake. Joe could hear his teeth chatter. 'You've killed Archie,' he said at last, forcing the words out. Vasco began to make sounds of sympathy but now Kevin had started he couldn't stop. 'You used him. Yes, you did. You used him like some poor little glove puppet. And now you've finished with him. And I'm supposed to hand over the pearl, am I? Well, forget it, Mr Shine. If you want your property that bad, you'll have to fry *me* with your fancy lightning, 'cos that's the only way you're ever going to get it!'

Vasco reached inside his jacket for his watch. 'It was an accident, Kevin,' he said gently. 'You must believe me. I wouldn't knowingly hurt Archie. He's a great little dog.'

'*Was*,' said Kevin, his chin wobbling violently. 'Was a great dog. Anyway, how would you know?' he glared.

'Believe it or not,' said Vee, 'I grew quite fond of him. He has – had – real spirit. I really enjoyed all his funny little memories. And he absolutely worshipped you, Kevin. But you must see how important this is,' he continued smoothly. 'I have to have the pearl. I really have to.'

'Nah, you don't,' said Kevin, his face twisting with hatred. ''Cos you don't deserve it. So save your sweet-talk. I don't want it, or nothing else you've got. All I want is Archie and he's gone now. It's no use you creeping up all incey-wincey, neither,' he warned, seeing Vasco moving stealthily towards him. ' 'Cos all I'll do then is I'll just chuck it in the river, all right?'

Vee passed his hand across his face. 'You're not

making this easy, Kevin. Don't force me to do some-thing we'll both regret.'

'I told you,' said Kevin, strangely calm, 'you can't touch me now, Vee, 'cos I've got nothing left to lose. You've lost the game.'

'I don't really think I have, you know.'

There was a squeak of terror and suddenly Vee had his arm tightly round Flora. 'I think our game was more complicated than you realised. Now, please, Kevin. Once and for all, let me have the pearl.'

'Don't,' said Flora through chattering teeth. 'Run as fast as you can and give it to Alice. Don't give in to him.'

Kevin looked up, white-faced, at the ship where Alice and the rangers watched helplessly, forbidden to interfere.

Vee tightened his grip and Flora moaned with fear.

'I'm sorry, Alice,' cried Kevin, 'but I can't let him.' In a stumbling rush, he thrust the pearl at Vee. Flora fled across to Joe and threw her arms round him.

Kevin crouched down and carefully gathered Archie into his arms. Now Archie had left it behind, his empty body sagged like a pathetic little pyjama case. Joe couldn't bear to see it. Flora wept as if her heart would break. But when Kevin looked up, his eyes were dry. Everything had been drained out of him, thought Joe. Even tears.

'Well, you got what you wanted, Vee,' he said quietly. 'So now do us all a favour. Turn yourself into a blooming butterfly and fly away, why don'tcha!'

But Vasco just stood gazing blankly at the pearl, which contained every dream his vampire father stole from him, as if he was wondering why he still felt so empty. And Joe saw it dawn on Vee that it was too late. That though he held them in his hand at last, he would never know for sure now, what those dreams were.

Vee stared at the children with their tired, frightened faces. Then he looked in a kind of dread at the bedraggled dead dog he had been. And it must have unlocked some fearful memory because, with a cry of horror, Vee drew back his hand and hurled the pearl into the river. He ripped the watch furiously from its chain and hurled it further still. Then he covered his face with his hands.

No one moved or spoke or looked at anyone. Everything they had longed for, all they had dreamed of, had vanished and there was nothing anyone could do. Their quest was over. It was the worst moment of their lives.

Then the whispers began.

Not in the river, or in this or that part of the dream fields, but everywhere at once, like a summer shower. The tiny restless sounds came from the dream fields

171

themselves. As the whispers grew, the children looked up, puzzled. Little flickers and glimmers of sound darted round them, softer than sunlight, kinder than rain. In their passing, these airy presences lightly touched a child here or a muddy dog there. But this was just in passing, for they were intent on one thing and one thing only.

The little breezy sounds went on twirling and swirling themselves into the gentlest, most persistent of whirlwinds, uttering feathery sighs and soft loving exclamations, until Vee raised his head, his eyes dark with bewilderment. And it seemed Vee and the whirlwind once knew each other, for he whispered, 'Is it you?' Impulsively, not knowing why he did it, Vee held out his open palm. And his stolen dreams flew into it and became part of him again.

But it was what happened after he got his dreams back that told Joe for certain that Vasco Shine's dream-snatching days were truly over. In two strides he was at Kevin's side. He dropped to his knees and quickly felt Archie's chest. 'Kevin,' Vee told him urgently, 'I think your little dog is still alive.'

14 Kevin Kitchener's dream

Vee said he'd make his own way home. 'I've got a few loose ends to tie up,' he said.

'Yes,' agreed Alice, her grey eyes soft. 'I expect you have.'

And at last Joe was dragging himself up a familiar rope ladder. He was dimly aware of Spinner bellowing instructions and that first electric quiver of the *Pineapple* as she began her terrifying shift. But, this time, as the dream fields slipped behind him in a blaze of beautiful blue, Joe crumpled into an exhausted sleep and somehow missed the whole thing.

Later, sensing the ship slow down, Joe groggily lifted his head and saw Alice gently taking Flora's baby sister from the arms of her mysterious babysitter.

As the strange creature bent its head over the sleepy little girl for one last look, Joe drowsily recognised delicate fronds, like something on an old lady's hat. Then he glimpsed a familiar palace with shining stairs, and grinned. Tat had been with Joe's old friend the monster all the time.

'Her cough is much better,' the monster murmured. 'And I only let her play with the more reliable mermaids.' Joe didn't catch what else he and Alice said to each other but, just before he fell back into a deep sleep, he felt strange rubbery fingers lovingly stroke his hair.

When Alice gently shook him awake again, it was so Joe could say his goodbyes.

'I hope you find your little girls soon, Spinner,' said Joe, throwing his arms around him. 'And, you know, you should really go and sing those songs to Finty, one of these days,' he told Lyle. 'Maybe you could go home once in a while,' he suggested shyly to Starbone. 'So you don't catch that horrible fever too often.'

But the little cook just swept Joe into a huge hug before he could say a word. When Floss put him down again, Joe was back in Forest Street, his teeth chattering with cold. Of course, it's winter here, he thought. But as he stood drowsily watching Kevin let himself in his front door, Joe saw that every trace of fog had gone.

'Heavens, I nearly forgot,' gasped Alice. 'There's one last thing we've got to do before your parents come home.' And she briskly hurried them along the dark silent street. What could she mean? Joe wondered.

'This is it,' said Alice breathlessly. 'Flora, hold Tat, please.'

They were outside some kind of shop. Its lights were on so Joe could see inside, where all kinds of renovations were underway. Upstairs a pretty blonde girl was stripping off great ribbons of wallpaper. At the front of the shop, a lanky boy vigorously bashed at some old plaster, raising clouds of dust. Music was playing somewhere. Joe could hear the girl singing along, slightly out of tune.

Alice knocked on the window. 'Is he here?' she called through the glass.

The youth opened the door. It was Jason Kitchener, Joe saw with surprise. 'Yeah, he just got back,' Jason told her. 'Oi, Vee,' he yelled. 'Young lady to see you.'

Joe and Flora exchanged astonished looks.

Vasco came out, drying his hands. Joe noticed paint in his hair.

'We forgot something,' Alice told him.

Vee looked puzzled. 'But I returned everything as soon as I got home.' Joe could see he was upset to think Alice didn't believe him.

'You're sure you sent back absolutely everything?' she insisted.

Suddenly Vee clapped his hand to his forehead in dismay. 'Is it too late?' he asked.

'If we're quick we should just get her through in time,' said Alice. 'Luna,' she called coaxingly. 'Time to go home!'

There was a frantic scrabbling of claws, then Vee's dog burst through the shop, wild with excitement. Alice glanced up and down the deserted street. 'We shouldn't really do this here, but I won't tell if you don't,' she told Luna.

Vee and Alice hurriedly traced a small door in the air, just large enough for a moonhound to get through. With a howl of joy, Luna hurled herself at the imaginary door and vanished in a beautiful blaze of blue.

'Of course,' breathed Joe. Vee's strange pedigree dog had been a moonhound all along.

'Floss will think he's gone to heaven when she turns up,' said Flora gleefully.

'At least one ranger had his dream come true,' Joe whispered, thinking of Spinner's search for his little girls.

'What's this place going to be when it's finished?' Alice was asking politely.

Vee shrugged. 'A café, or a music shop, maybe. I'm not sure yet. Well,' he said, a little shyly. 'Better get cracking. I'll see you around.'

And Alice Fazackerley hurried the children back home.

As she tucked him into bed, Joe asked her, 'Alice, did *you* know it was the dream fields all the time?'

She gave him a light kiss on his brow and he caught the scent of night in her hair. 'In this world, most people don't believe in dreams,' she said softly. 'So it's just as well dreams go on believing in us, isn't it?'

But Joe had a slight sense of being cheated. He was really happy Vasco had got his dreams back and everything. But he couldn't help feeling it was unfair the dream fields hadn't found a way to let the children bring back the Pearl of the Deep to their own world. Without the pearl itself, their quest felt somehow unfinished.

Then, minutes later, he heard voices downstairs.

'Alice really cuts it fine,' Flora giggled from her side of the room.

Joe heard his mum say, 'What a lovely smell there

177

is in your house, Tom. It reminds me of something, but I can't think what.'

Then Flora's dad's voice floated across the landing. 'Tat's cough seems much better,' he said, sounding surprised. 'Your Alice doesn't have magic powers does she?' he chuckled. Then his voice changed. 'What have you got there, sweetheart?'

Joe almost stopped breathing.

'Nyeugh stoppit. Bite you, Daddy,' a sleepy voice protested. 'Pretty pretty pretty mines.'

'Is it valuable, do you think?' Flora's dad asked. 'It looks very unusual.'

'I don't know,' said Joe's mum in a tone of wonder. 'I don't think I've seen a real pearl before.' Then she whispered, 'Tom, I've just peeped in at Joe. I think he's fast asleep. It seems such a shame to wake him.'

'Let him stay. I'll bring him back in the morning. Who knows?' murmured Tom Neate. 'Maybe he'll even get to like being here.'

And though Joe couldn't see her, he could *feel* Flora smiling in the dark. 'We brought it back after all,' he whispered, with a rush of joy.

'I know,' she said sleepily.

'Oh, *you* would, Flora Neate,' he told her.

Then they both turned over and fell asleep.

There was one more thing to be given back. Though

when Kevin Kitchener's dream finally arrived he didn't remember it at first.

It was a summer Saturday. As there was nothing to get up for, Kevin just lay in bed, feeling the reassuring weight of a snoozing Archie on his feet, vaguely listening to the noisy comings and goings across the landing. But as he lay there, not thinking about anything in particular, little scarcely visible scraps and wisps began to twirl together in his mind. And when they'd finished, there was a dream there. Nothing earth-shaking. It wasn't a big deal or anything but it gave Kevin a happy little buzz to know that Finty's infallible was just as infallible as she said it was.

He had dreamed, as it happened, about Finty's shack. Only, instead of Finty, his sister Karen was there, plumping up dozens of huge red, heart-shaped cushions. Suddenly she looked up and gave him a really sweet grin. 'Did you miss me, Kev?' she said. Then someone dropped something heavy outside his door and he woke with a jump.

The only trouble with dreaming was that it left you with a bit of an ache inside. Did he miss Karen? Not much I don't, he thought wistfully. Not blooming much.

Then it finally filtered through to Kevin that something odd was going on. The bumps and bangs had stopped for the time being. Downstairs someone started briskly searching through the kitchen cupboards. The

179

fridge door closed with a dull thunk. A bouncy reggae song blared through the house, until someone quickly turned the radio down.

Kevin sniffed the air. Toast, he thought. Someone's in our kitchen making toast. 'Come on, boy,' he said. Archie jumped off the bed and dashed obligingly after him.

As Kevin headed for the stairs, he noticed his sister's door standing open. Someone had dumped several large boxes inside, next to a couple of bulging suitcases. Three of the drawers in the chest of drawers stuck out at crazy angles. And as he stared at all this, it slowly dawned on Kevin that what he was witnessing was a sort of burglary in reverse.

Then he noticed the roughly tied parcel. Spilling out of it right across Karen's bed, was a bundle of bright red cushions which had burst their string.

He went thundering down the stairs at such a rate that he missed at least half of them.

In the kitchen, a dark-haired girl was trying to remove slices of toast from the toaster.

She'd been a red-head last time Kevin saw her. But apart from her hair, his sister looked just the same.

'She hasn't fixed the toaster, I see,' Karen remarked.

'I'll do it,' said Kevin huskily. 'You need a bit of a knack.'

Karen blew on her scorched fingers. 'You need a new toaster,' she said.

He was still staring at her. 'I thought you'd left home.'

'That didn't work out. Shall I put some in for you, while I'm at it?' She sat down and started hungrily on her breakfast.

'So, are you back then?' he asked, as if he was just casually inquiring.

Karen licked jam off her finger. 'It depends,' she said vaguely. She went back to studying a poster Jason had stuck up for some reason, advertising some kind of family day in the park. 'Want to walk up and take a look later, when I've sorted my room out?' she asked. Then suddenly she flashed him a sweet grin. 'Did you miss me, Kev?'

It was afternoon by the time Kevin and his sister made it to the park. But before they reached the gates, an eerie sighing sound made him glance up warily.

A brightly patterned balloon was floating over their heads, then a few seconds afterwards a brilliant yellow one appeared over the rooftops. But it wasn't until he was actually inside the park that Kevin realised Karen had brought him to some kind of balloon festival.

It reminded him of a fair, with the milling crowd and bright colours, the smell of grass and fried onions.

And he didn't mind being there or anything, but he was faintly surprised Karen had suggested it, when she had things to do at home.

Karen queued for choc-ices and then the two of them strolled about, trying to eat them before they melted in the sun. He recognised dozens of kids from school and even a couple of teachers. This festival was a bigger deal than he'd realised.

'It's good this, isn't it?' said Karen happily. 'I'm dead proud of him, Kevin, aren't you?'

But he couldn't think who she meant.

There were balloons everywhere, busily arriving and leaving. And there was something so familiar about the scene, that suddenly Kevin thought he knew who might be behind it.

He caught sight of Joe in the crowd. 'I wondered where you'd got to,' said Joe. 'Hiya, Karen.'

'She's back home for a while,' said Kevin. 'It was her idea to come here really.'

'Flora's dad's trying to persuade Mum to come up in one with us,' Joe sighed. 'But she says someone should look after Tat. That's Flora's baby sister,' he explained to Karen.

'Oh, why don't I take her?' cried Karen at once. To Kevin's alarm she went diving into the crowd. The next time he caught sight of her glossy dark head, she was cheerfully introducing herself to someone.

'Karen's a girl who makes things happen,' he explained.

'I can tell,' said Joe.

Kevin gestured to the balloon-filled sky. 'Vasco Shine wouldn't have anything to do with this, would he?'

'Didn't you know?' said Joe surprised. 'He and your brother have been organising it for weeks.' He grinned. 'Here have this. Jason's giving them to everyone in sight!'

'What's this then, when it's at home?' said Kevin, examining the little card with a baffled scowl.

'Their balloon company, stupid,' said Joe. Then he shook his head. 'Don't you *ever* talk to each other at your house, Kevin?'

But Kevin was still staring at the little card. There it was in black and white:

Dream Catchers.
Makers of quality hot air balloons.
Vasco Shine and Jason Kitchener

Suddenly Kevin heard what Joe had said. 'No,' he said gruffly. 'The Kitcheners don't chat a great deal.'

Karen came back breathlessly pushing a buggy with a very pale baby in it. Tat was asleep, Kevin saw with relief.

'They're going any minute,' Karen told Joe. 'You'd better run or they'll leave you behind.' Joe dashed excitedly into the crowd.

'Why don't you go, Kev?' Karen suggested. 'I'm sure they could squeeze you in.'

He shook his head. 'Nah,' he said. 'I tried ballooning once. Didn't like it.'

And suddenly there was Vee, carefully helping someone into a balloon. The girl turned her head and with a flash of delight Kevin recognised Alice. Vee said something to her and she waved to Kevin and he waved back.

Then their balloon floated up and away into the summer sky.

And as Kevin stood in the sunshine, it suddenly came to him exactly what all this busy magical coming and going reminded him of.

It's like the dream fields, he thought in amazement. But he couldn't really say that to Karen. So he said casually, 'Karen, what would you say if I told you that pale sweet little sleeping baby you're cooing over there was really a vampire?'

Then when his sister's mouth fell open, he staggered all over the grass, laughing like a hyena.

'Just kidding, Karen,' said Kevin, grinning his famous grin. 'Just kidding.'